RECON

Panic seized the rest of the expedition. Two women, one nearly naked, ran for the jungle. One stumbled. As she looked up, she saw her friend lifted off her feet and thrown through the air, a cloud of blood following her like a crimson vapor trail. Hughes burst from his tent, a survival rifle in his hand. But he didn't raise or aim it. There were no targets visible, just a howling from the jungle around them.

Those who still lived were frozen, unable to act or to think. They were waiting for death to seize them as it had the others.

SEALS

SEALS

#7

RECON

STEVE MACKENZIE

AVON BOOKS ◆ NEW YORK

SEALS #7: RECON is an original publication of Avon Books. This work has never before appeared in book form. This work is a novel. Any similarity to actual persons or events is purely coincidental.

AVON BOOKS
A division of
The Hearst Corporation
105 Madison Avenue
New York, New York 10016

First Avon Books Printing: May 1988

AVON TRADEMARK REG. U.S. PAT. OFF. AND IN OTHER COUNTRIES, MARCA REGISTRADA, HECHO EN U.S.A.

Printed in the U.S.A.

K–R   10   9   8   7   6   5   4   3   2   1

1

The driving beat of the drums drifted through the morning mist, a sound that was heard on a subliminal level. Something that couldn't be heard unless listened for, but there, nagging, like a minor toothache. Brian Moore, a large, robust man dressed in khaki and with flaming red hair, a handlebar mustache, and a goatee, sat on the rotting log in the green hell of the Honduran jungle and tried to hear the drums over the rattling of the leaves and the scrambling of the monkeys and the lizards. Although he couldn't tell much about it, he knew he didn't like it. There was something sinister about the sound, something evil.

Moore turned and looked into the small clearing on top of the plateau where the camp had been set up. There were bright orange tents, dome-shaped affairs that could easily hold two or three cots, or a cot and some kind of collapsible, lightweight field desk. The six tents had been erected in a circle, the entrances facing in. A fire had burned in the middle of them throughout the night but was now just smoking remains. Other equipment—lanterns, shovels, a military mine detector that was little more than a glorified metal detector—sat close to the fire, catching and reflecting the morning sun.

Sara Robinson crouched over a metal pot, stirring it with a thin stick. A tall, slender woman with long black hair tied back in a ponytail, she was a graduate student in archaeology with an emphasis on the high civilizations of Mesoamerica and the Central Andes. She wore khaki shorts rolled high, a khaki shirt, and sandals.

She pulled the stick from the water, shook it, and then tossed it to the side. She stood, put a hand up to shield her eyes, and then waved at Moore.

"I got the water hot for coffee," she called, her voice nearly lost in the chattering of the monkeys and the screaming of the birds.

And, under it all, the rumble of the drums. The quiet, distant rumble of the drums.

Moore stood, picked up the sapling he'd cut down and stripped for a walking stick, and hurried to the center of the camp. As he approached, he heard morning noises from the other tents as the rest of the expedition stirred.

"Coffee looks really awful," Moore said as he stared down into the pot.

Robinson shrugged. "What do you expect? It's not like I've got a percolator and household current."

"Don't be so defensive, Sara. The coffee'll be fine. Just don't let it boil."

He dipped the tin cup she handed him into the pot and lifted the steaming liquid toward his face. He inhaled deeply and felt like coughing, but he stifled the response. He blew on the top and tried it carefully so he wouldn't burn his tongue. The coffee wasn't nearly as bad as it looked.

Jason Hughes, a large young man who had once played football but who had gotten caught up in the academic end of the university, stumbled out of his tent. He had light skin, now sunburned, and dark, windblown hair. He raised both hands over his head, stretching and roaring. He wore khaki shorts and nothing else.

"That coffee?" he asked.

"Masquerades as it," said Moore, grinning.

"Then get me a cup." Suddenly he cocked his head: "What the hell is that? We in Africa?"

"I'm not sure exactly what it is or what it means," Moore said, staring into the jungle surrounding them. "I first heard it about midnight."

From another of the tents two more men appeared. Both were shorter and darker than the university people. These men, who claimed a knowledge of the interior, had been hired when the expedition had reached the Honduran coast. They could lead the Americans into the Honduran jungles and help them locate the lost city. More important, they could lead them out once the lost city was discovered.

They stayed away from the others as much as they could, talking to one another in a strange mix of Spanish and some local language. Crouched near the entrance to their tent, they had their heads cocked as if listening to something.

Hughes pointed at the two natives and asked, "What's with them?"

Moore dipped more coffee into his cup and then sat on the ground, his back against a log, his wrist resting on his knee. He glanced at the two men and shrugged.

More members of the expedition staggered into the bright morning sunlight, stretching and blinking. They were all attired in a variety of clothes that did little to cover them— shorts and shirts and sandals. Three men and three women, each moving toward the fire and the bubbling pot of coffee. Each of them seemed to hear the drums. Each would stop, listen for a moment, and then shrug.

Hughes, a cup in his hand, stood and looked into the distance. The land dropped away to the west so that he was looking over a sea green forest with wisps of light fog drifting among the giant trees. Low-hanging clouds threatened rain, although the sky was clear to the east.

There was a peacefulness to the scene, a quiet that made it seem as though they had traveled back through time until they stood in the jungle that the first natives had seen. There were no jets overhead, no power poles cutting through the territory. The jungle was unbroken and verdant as far as the eye could see.

The only blemish on the tranquil scene was the crackle and pop of the shortwave radio as Roger Bartel tried to establish contact with their home base at the university. He was speaking quietly, his words lost in the light breeze.

Under all that, was the ominous rumble of the drums with their haunting, evil rhythm that made Hughes nervous. He didn't like it, but couldn't explain why. Maybe it was because it suggested that the people living in the region knew that the expedition was there and were alerting others. Or maybe it was the subliminal nature of the sound: a constant beat that couldn't really be heard, a rumbling felt in the soles of the feet and in the teeth and in the air.

Hughes turned, moving toward his tent where his notebook lay. It contained questions that he wanted to send to the university. He wanted explanations for some of the strange things that they had seen and heard in the last few days—a lot of strange things that had nothing to do with the fact of their being in the jungle.

As he reached the flap of his tent, a strange whirring sound cut through the morning. Instinctively, he ducked and spun.

Bartel was turning toward the sound when his head seemed to explode. A crimson spray fountained into the morning as the headless torso sat upright for a second and then dropped to the ground. Blood spread outward from it in a quickly expanding pool.

Hughes was stunned. It was several seconds before he realized what he had seen. There was a scream. A terrified woman stood near the camp fire, her body rigid as she stared, screaming, at the remains of Bartel twitching on the ground in front of her.

Shouting erupted. The two native guides ran for the safety of the nearby jungle, neither looking back. Moore threw his coffee cup away and ran for his tent. He grabbed the flap and ducked to enter when something struck him in the back. The world around him turned black and he couldn't move. He collapsed to the ground.

Several other members of the expedition rushed into the bright morning light. Around them they heard the turmoil, but they could see nothing other than the headless body of Bartel and the prone shape of Moore. One of the men took a step toward the radio that was still crackling, but then he was hit. Blood blossomed on his chest. He stared at it dumbly, as if he couldn't understand what had happened. He sat down and rolled to his side as blood pumped from his chest.

Panic seized the rest of the expedition. Two women, one nearly naked, ran for the jungle. One of them stumbled, falling to her hands and knees. As she looked up, she saw her friend lifted off her feet and thrown through the air, a cloud of blood following her like a crimson vapor trail. There was no cry of pain or surprise as the woman hit the ground and rolled over. She didn't move.

Hughes burst from his tent, a survival rifle in his hand. It was a small thing, made of tubing and holding a clip with ten .22 caliber rounds in it. He didn't raise it or aim it. There were no targets visible. Just a howling that seemed to come from the jungle around them. Not a point source of noise, but a continuous band of racket surrounding them.

Those who still lived were frozen, unable to act or to think, simply waiting for death to seize them as it had the others.

Bruce Carrigan sat in front of the shortwave radio, a microphone in his hand and desperately tried to reestablish contact with the expedition. He sat there, staring at the panel with its glowing amber lights and dancing needles, waiting for someone to talk to him. Sweat dripped down his face and trickled down his sides as he studied the speaker, trying to will it to make noise.

He glanced at the clock and watched as the second hand crawled around the face. He listened to the carrier wave and knew that the radio at the other end still operated. But no one would answer his increasingly frantic calls. He flipped through the loose-leaf binder sitting on the table beside him, searching for the emergency procedures that everyone had thought a silly notion.

Standing next to him, her face a pasty white, was Jane Gauliff, who suddenly wanted to cry. Her eyes were on the dark cork that lined the interior of the small room to soundproof it. It absorbed the light, making the room dim. The odor of it filled the air. There were several maps pinned to it, one of them a giant chart of Honduras with the expedition's route of march drawn on it in bright red.

"What's going on down there?" she said quietly, her voice shaking.

Carrigan shrugged helplessly. She had heard, just as he had, the initial contact. Everything seemed to be fine then. A calm, routine report. Then screaming and strange sounds and finally nothing except the carrier wave.

Carrigan leaned closer and worked with the radio, slowly changing the frequency until the carrier wave noise disappeared. He rolled it back to the proper spot and made another attempt to raise the expedition. That failed, too.

Gauliff slipped into the folding metal chair, the only available seat and felt the sweat blossom as if the room had suddenly gotten ten degrees warmer. She felt her head swim and she wanted to do something, but didn't know what.

Carrigan shook his head. "I can't raise them. Maybe you'd better tell Dr. Thomas that we've lost radio contact with the team."

"Lost radio contact?" she said, her voice shrill. "Something attacked them!"

Carrigan turned to the young woman. Her face was bloodless and she looked scared, afraid for the fate of the expedition. He shook his head. "Now, we don't know that. There could be a dozen explanations for everything we heard.''

"Sure," she said, unconvinced.

"Until we have some more information, it'll do us no good to speculate. We can imagine all sorts of things, but until we have the information, we're wasting our time. You just go tell Dr. Thomas that radio communications have temporarily broken down.''

She stood but didn't move immediately to the door. She wiped a hand over her face and then examined the sweat smeared on her palm. ''Those people were being killed down there and you'd better do something about that now.''

Carrigan stared into her eyes and asked, ''Just what would you have me do? They're five thousand miles away stuck in a jungle. There is nothing that I can do.''

2

Naval Lieutenant Mark Tynan was finally having a good time. It had been a while since the last opportunity because his assignments in the SEALS had kept him out of the country, trying not to get killed. And when he wasn't doing that, he was in training, trying to learn the best that the British SAS, among others, had to offer. He had trained with the Israelis and the West Germans and the South Vietnamese. Finally tiring of all that, he looked at his military service jacket and realized that he'd accumulated a great deal of leave time. He decided to take it and return to the United States with its all-night generators.

Tynan, a young man nearing thirty, had been in the Navy for almost seven years. He had joined just after college, and gone to sea on a cruiser. Then he heard about the SEALS and decided that it would be more exciting than standing on the bridge of a ship directing artillery fire at shore targets, never getting to see them blow up.

Now, back in the States, his brown hair cropped short so everyone could identify him as military, he was on leave—a visit home to see his mother and father and then his old high-school and college friends. He had been drinking in the local bars, having some of the men buy him beers because he had been to Vietnam, and others refusing to talk to him because he had been to Vietnam.

8

Not that he cared about the politics of the situation. As an officer in the armed forces of the United States, politics was not his major interest. He just went where they told him to go, did what they told him to do, and tried to survive it. It was not the best-paying career in the world, but it sure was exciting as hell.

After two weeks, he was beginning to get tired of his leave. Somehow, all the people he talked to, all the women he dated, missed the essence of the war in Vietnam or the purpose of a military force. All of them, regardless of political orientation, thought that it was the Pentagon that went out searching for fights. Generals and admirals, trying to justify their existence, wanted to get into a shooting war. When a major conflict was not available, a little one would do.

The funny thing was that everyone seemed to think that after they told Tynan about the flaws in military thinking, he would rush back to his billet and inform those in higher positions. No one understood that he had nothing to do with establishing policy. Policy was the bailiwick of Congress and the president, not the military.

Because of all that, Tynan had decided to ignore everyone for a night and head out on his own in search of fun. Hit a few bars where he would know no one, have a late dinner somewhere, and then catch the last feature at the movies. An anonymous evening that allowed him to forget about everything for a few hours and concentrate on having fun.

At the tavern he sat at the bar, a glass of beer in front of him and the news playing on the color television. The pinball machines to the left, set in an alcove, popped and buzzed and rang while the men playing them shouted encouragement at one another. In the booths scattered along the wall, couples sat drinking quietly, talking to one another. The jukebox belted out the latest song from the Beatles or the Rolling Stones, drowning out the sound from the TV. Tynan watched the people on the screen reading the news (or becoming the news) as they tried to report it. He didn't really care what was being said.

Tynan grabbed a handful of beer nuts and popped them into his mouth. On the screen, the reporter was interviewing a woman standing outside one of the buildings at some university. She looked upset and Tynan figured that students, in the name of freedom, had taken over another of the campus's buildings. On tomorrow's news, the police would be seen dragging the offenders off to jail in the name of freedom.

He felt a hand on his shoulder and turned to stare into a pair of deep blue eyes. "Susan!"

"I thought that you was you, Mark. What are you doing down in this neck of the woods?"

He slipped off the stool so that he was standing next to her. She was a tall woman, five foot seven or eight, with long straight hair parted in the middle, and tiny hands. The features of her face were fine, though her nose was just a little pointed. It was the only flaw. Her wide-set eyes of a deep, dark blue more than made up for it.

"Can I buy you a beer?" he asked.

She took the stool next to him, her short skirt riding up her thigh as she sat down. She leaned both elbows on the bar and smiled at herself in the mirror behind it.

"Beer always makes me sleepy, and besides that, I don't like it that much. I'd like a martini, dry, with a twist."

Tynan slipped back onto his stool and stole a glance at her. "You've come quite a way from a glass of beer and a handful of pretzels."

"I think we've all had the chance to grow up in the last couple of years," she said misinterpreting his remark. Now she turned to face him. "Given what's going on around us, it's hard not to have grown up."

The bartender moved close and Tynan ordered the drinks. As the man stepped to the side to make them, Tynan said,

"We seem to have gotten ourselves into a couple of messes recently."

Now she stared at him—at his short, dark hair, the deep tan that suggested he'd been in an environment that was not as cold and dark as that in the local area. She noticed the new scar on his chin that was a puckered white.

"I see that your political beliefs haven't changed since college."

The bartender dropped off the drinks, setting each on a little napkin. Tynan handed him a ten and watched him head to the cash register with it. When he had delivered the change, Tynan responded to Susan.

"I never had any political beliefs. Like everyone else in college, I was preparing for my career."

She drank half her martini in one gulp and didn't flinch. She stuck a finger into the drink to swirl it around. "That career include killing women and children?"

"Hey, Susan. What is this? 'Killing women and children.' Where in the hell did that come from?"

"Sorry about that," she said. She raised her glass and finished her drink. "It's the news from the war. I'm so sick of hearing about how many people were killed today. How many American boys died, and how many Vietnamese, and how many civilians."

"It's a terrible thing," said Tynan.

"And you participate in it," she accused suddenly.

For an instant, Tynan was too surprised to answer. Then he grinned and said, "Not all that recently. Besides, it's the only war we have."

The color drained from her face and her mouth pumped as she fought to think of something to say.

The grin never left Tynan's face. He held up a hand, as if to ward off a blow and said, "Makes as much sense as anything you say."

"I thought I could talk to you on a rational level," she snapped.

"You didn't want to talk about it," said Tynan, suddenly angry. "You wanted to lecture. You wanted me to sit here and listen to your half-baked notions and political commentary, and let it go."

She opened her purse and dug through it, tossing things on the bar until she located a couple of dollar bills. She put them next to the empty martini glass. As she shoveled everything back into her purse, she said, "I'll buy my own drink, thank you very much."

Tynan ducked his head in a mock bow and said, "You do what you think is right."

"At least I *do think*," she hissed.

"So that's what you call it," he said, wondering how the conversation had turned ugly so quickly.

"Brilliant answer," she said. "But then, I'd expect that from someone who would be in the same army with the men who killed women and children at My Lai."

"What about the five thousand killed by the VC and NVA at Hue? Don't they rate your sympathy?"

"It's not the same thing," she said, her voice rising as she slapped the bar with an open hand.

"It's exactly the same thing: innocent women and children—and men—dead by violence, but no one in this country wants to hear a thing about it because it justifies our involvement in the war."

"Just as the bodies at My Lai justify it?" she asked, sneering.

"A terrible and tragic incident and we'll learn something about our government when the men responsible are brought to trial. And there we see the difference. We'll hold ourselves accountable for that act of terror, but the enemy won't for the deaths of the people at Hue."

"You fascist," she spat as she turned and stormed from the tavern.

As she hit the front door, the bartender arrived to pick up the empty glass and the money. He used a damp towel to clean the bar and asked, "What'd you say to her?"

"Never talk politics or religion to a woman," said Tynan quietly.

"I thought you would have learned that by now," said the bartender.

"She brought up the subject. I thought she wanted to have a discussion."

"Man, where have you been lately? They don't want discussion."

Tynan looked at the television and saw that the same woman was on the screen. He pointed and said, "What happened there? The students burn down a building in the name of higher education?"

The bartender turned and looked, one hand on his hip. "Nah. They lost some scientific expedition in South America or something. Been on the news all day. You ready for another of those?"

Tynan looked at his nearly empty glass. Suddenly, he didn't feel like drinking another beer. In fact, he no longer felt like eating dinner or seeing a movie. All he wanted to do was head home. The thought of all those strangers around him was almost too much to bear.

"No thanks. Think I'll pack it in."

"Well, good night to you, then. And say. The next time a good-looking woman sits down with you, you agree with her, even if she tells you the sky is green and the grass is blue."

He climbed off his stool and stood there for a moment, searching through his wallet. He found a couple of singles and tossed them on the bar. "Thanks for the advice."

The bartender stuffed the bills into a glass sitting nearby and nodded his head. "Thank you."

Dr. William Thomas sat at the head of the highly polished table whose massiveness suggested its heritage was in the nineteenth century. It was an old, well-used, well-built table that was now the centerpiece of the conference room for the Department of Anthropology and Antiquities at the university. The other, more glamorous departments had the new chrome-and-glass look, but the anthropologists seemed to like the image of the last century.

Sitting in there with him were Bruce Carrigan and his graduate assistant, Jane Gauliff. Next to them were Drs. Sally Foster, Timothy Hardgroves, and Stephanie King. There were two graduate students on the other side of the table and one at the door. All of them looked shaken. The shock of losing the expedition was beginning to set in and the implications of that scared each of them.

Thomas could stand it no more. He got to his feet and walked to the windows, huge floor-to-ceiling things that had been fashionable fifty years earlier, when the building was erected. He looked out on the darkened campus, at the pools of light created by the lampposts that belonged in a Sherlock Holmes mystery. Although they looked like gaslights, they were electric and they added an eerie, unreal feeling to the somber mood of the room.

Still facing the windows, Thomas said, "It would take us a week or more, maybe as long as three or four, to get someone in there to learn what has happened. Much too long. We must act on this now."

"But we don't want to go off half-cocked," cautioned Hardgroves.

"Tim, you didn't hear the sounds over the radio. If we're going to send someone in, we're going to have to do it quickly because I don't know how long the expedition can survive," said Carrigan.

"If there are any survivors," added Gauliff.

Thomas spun and faced them. "We don't need that kind of talk now. Of course there are survivors. We have lost radio contact under suspicious circumstances, but there is no need to postulate the extermination of our people."

"What course of action will we pursue?" asked King. She was a young woman, having received her doctorate the semester before. Her position on the staff had come about because of her intelligence and dedication, plus a brilliant desertation on the Mayans.

Thomas returned to his seat and opened one of the file folders sitting in front of him. He studied the map and shook his head. "The university does not have the resources required to mount a second expedition."

"And we don't have the talent," Gauliff said.

"What does that mean?" asked Thomas.

Gauliff could feel her career in anthropology slipping away from her. Her scientific detachment had deserted her when she had heard the cries of fear and pain over the radio followed by that ominous silence.

"It means," she said, "that we need someone who understands the jungle and who knows how to protect himself. We need someone familiar with firearms."

"You're becoming a bit melodramatic," Thomas said, shaking his head slowly.

"I'm trying to be realistic," she countered. "A hundred years ago, these expeditions were mounted with guides and explorers who understood the jungles and the use of rifles. Now we go off into the jungle like it's a walk through the Black Forest."

"Jane," said Carrigan, "you're out of line here."

"Out of line or not, I think that we've stumbled onto something that we're not equipped to handle. I think we should contact the State Department, tell them everything we know and let them handle it."

"That'll take days to arrange," said one of the graduate students.

"And if we continue the way we're going," said Jane, "it'll take *weeks*. We need action now, not two weeks from now. We need action when there is still a hope that we can find our people."

"There is a possibility," said Carrigan, "that we could arrange an overflight of the area. I have a friend with a twin engine aircraft . . ."

"No," said Thomas. "I think we're too far away."

"He can fly down in short legs, refueling frequently, and never have to fly over water. He could land in Tegucigalpa to refuel and then have plenty of range."

Thomas was quiet as he studied a map of Central America. He shook his head and said, "I can't see it. There's too much territory, and a single plane with a single pilot doesn't seem to be an adequate response."

"But he can be airborne and on his way tomorrow morning. There's no one else who could do that."

Thomas looked at the people in the room with him and shook his head again. "Maybe he could be airborne tomorrow but he won't have the flight clearances, and if someone refuses him overflight permission, then he'd have to detour over water. He might not get landing permission when he needs it or takeoff clearances once he's on the ground. This is an amateur effort. We need something more professional."

"So," said Carrigan sarcastically, "we call the State Department and they call the ambassador in Honduras, who contacts the government there, who finally dispatches someone who *might* actually go out to look."

Thomas took a deep breath and rubbed a hand through his thick, white, wavy hair. "No. We contact State and tell them what we know and what we suspect, but we keep our options open."

"How soon?" asked Carrigan.

Thomas closed the file folder in front of him. "As soon as we wrap it up here, I'll speak to the president of the university, outlining a course of action. We'll make the calls as quickly as possible."

Carrigan stood up, the legs of his chair scraping on the hardwood floor. "I don't think we're doing enough about this."

"That might be," Thomas said, "but right now, there isn't much else we can do. We'll have to wait for morning anyway, so we'll delay until then. A few hours one way or the other won't make any difference. Is there anything else that anyone would like to say?" he asked as he stood.

"Only that it's just like everything else at this university," said Cauliff. "We'll give it to a committee to study so that we don't have to make a decision."

"Jane, I know you're upset so I'm going to ignore that remark. Now does anyone have anything constructive to add? No? Then I'll see you all here tomorrow at nine."

Thomas left the conference room rapidly, hurried down the dimly lighted corridor lined with display cases holding dioramas from the past: an ancient Indian village; samples of stone tools from Africa; a chart showing the patterns of evolution.

He left the building, turned right, and walked toward the president's house at the far end of the campus, where the man waited for information. Thomas wished that he had some to give him.

Tynan pulled his Mustang into the driveway and turned off the engine and the lights. He glanced upward into the sky, which was ablaze with stars. The slash of the Milky Way was obvious and the moon, dropping close to the horizon, was a deep orange.

He walked up to the front door, where the porch light burned, and opened it. His father sat in the living room, watching the late news. "Home so soon? I thought you were going to stay out."

"Couldn't find a movie worth going to." He sat on the couch and watched the news for a moment and then said, "I think I'll head up to bed."

His father turned and said, "Everything okay?"

Tynan grinned. "Everything's just fine. I'm tired and it's a real luxury to have a bed with clean sheets instead of a nest on a jungle floor or a hammock tied in a tree."

"Well, I'm going to have a beer before I turn in. How about you?"

"Then it looks like I'm going to have to have one,

too.'' Tynan leaned back and studied the room. It was alive with memories: Santa Claus setting up an electric train for Christmas. The prom night as he stood in the ill-fitting tux that his mother had rented for him that morning. Fights with his brother and sister. Walking in on his sister and her boyfriend as they explored each other's naked body. All kinds of interesting memories. And in case the memories somehow faded, pictures on the walls and on the mantel.

His father returned with the beer and sat down facing his son. He glanced at the floor and said, ''You having a good time here?''

''Sure.'' He shrugged and took a drink of the beer.

''You have a steady girl?''

''A steady girl?'' repeated Tynan. ''What is this? I'm not in high school. I know a couple of women and like them well enough, but my job tends to limit my social life somewhat. You fishing for some grandkids here?''

''Well, you're not getting any younger.''

''I have a brother and a sister who can provide all the grandkids you need for the next couple of years. In fact, I'm surprised that they haven't had a few already.''

''Now, don't go getting mad at me. I'm only asking because you never tell us anything about what you do.''

Feeling that he was on solid ground, he said, ''That's only because I'm not supposed to talk about it. At least, not the details. You know I'm in the Navy.''

''But that's no career.''

''Sure it is. Hell, Dad, thousands of men have made the military their careers. There's nothing wrong with that, is there?''

''No. I just wondered if you'd thought beyond the immediate future. Getting out of the Navy and taking a nice job around here.''

''Doing what? Selling insurance or real estate? Dad, I like what I'm doing and I'm very good at it. People respect me for what I do.''

"Not around here."

Tynan felt the anger flare as it had in the bar when Susan started talking about the war and politics; then, suddenly, he just felt tired. "That mean you and Mom and the family, or does it mean someone else?"

"You know that your mother and I are proud of everything that you've accomplished in your life. Some of the neighbors who have boys getting very close to draft age have made a few comments."

Tynan drained his beer and leaned back, resting his head against the wall—something his mother had told him not to do a hundred different times.

"Well, given the circumstances, I can't say that I blame them, but they've got to realize that all this Vietnam business is not my fault." He stopped for a moment and then added, "You know that this is the second time tonight I've had to make that speech?"

"You know that I'm not criticizing . . ."

"Sure. I know that."

The phone rang then. Both could hear it in the back of the house. They only had one phone, a black one hanging on the wall in the kitchen near the back door. They heard Tynan's mother answer it. As Tynan glanced at his watch he caught the look of alarm on his father's face.

"Hey, relax. It can't be all that bad. If it was, they'd have sent someone."

Tynan's mother appeared and said, "It's for Mark." She dropped her voice and said, "It's someone in the Pentagon. Some captain or commander or someone. It sounded official."

"If they're calling this late at night, it's official. I'll go take it."

Tynan walked through the dining room and into the kitchen. He plucked the receiver off the counter and closed his eyes, steeling himself for the bad news. "This is Lieutenant Tynan."

"Lieutenant, we've a bit of a flap going over at State

and wondered if you could attend a meeting tomorrow at eleven hundred hours our time.''

Tynan looked at the clock hanging over the aqua-colored refrigerator. It had a red plaid design that clashed with the refrigerator and the wall.

"Might be cutting it close. Depends on the flight arrangements but I should be able to make it if I leave now. What about orders?"

"They're being cut now. This is a verbal authorization. You'll need to give your flight information to my office and I'll detail someone to pick you up at the airport."

Tynan closed his eyes again and took a deep breath. "Let me get a pencil for the specifics."

"Make it snappy, Lieutenant."

"Yes, sir."

3

The officer on the phone had been as good as his word. There was a driver and car waiting for him when his plane landed at Washington's National Airport. The driver, a Marine corporal, had singled Tynan out and then led him through the terminal to the luggage carousel and finally out the main doors into the massive, car-choked parking lot where the government vehicle waited.

They drove out from the airport, past the Pentagon, where Tynan was sure they would go for the meetings, and into the city itself. They wound their way past buildings that were symbols of U.S. heritage—the Lincoln Memorial, the Washington Monument, the White House—until they could look up and see the Capitol. They pulled up in front of a high rise building of glass and steel. A man slipped from the doorway and stepped briskly to the car. He opened the rear door so that Tynan could exit.

After Tynan got out, the car roared off. Since his seabag was in the trunk, he hoped that the driver was looking for a parking lot. He watched it disappear down a side street, and then let the doorman lead him into the lobby.

There a uniformed guard holding a clipboard asked, "And you are?"

"Lieutenant Mark Tynan."

"Yes, sir." He consulted his list and said, "You're to

meet with the people in room D-402 on the fourth floor.''
He turned and took a badge from the board behind him.
''Please wear this at all times and do not stray from the
fourth floor.''

Tynan clipped the green, laminated badge to his pocket
and noted the big black four on it. He walked to the
elevator and when the door opened got in. The woman
standing at the controls said nothing other than, ''Fourth
floor coming up.'' She grinned at him as she hit the
button.

When the elevator reached the fourth floor, Tynan got
out. He stood in a large lobby of bright orange. The walls
were covered with burnt orange and there was orange
carpeting on the floor. Gold letters on the wall told him
where he wanted to go. He found the conference room and
opened the door.

The inside looked like a hundred other conference rooms:
a large table surrounded by chairs, a screen recessed into
the ceiling at the far end, and a wet bar to one side.

The furniture and table were high quality and more
expensive than usual for a Navy conference room.

There were ten people inside, three of them women and
seven men. All looked as if they had been struck from the
same mold. They all wore buttoned-down collars and gray
suits. The only difference was that the women wore skirts.

One of the men stood and waved Tynan into the room.
He pointed to the vacant chair and asked, ''Are you the
Navy guy who's supposed to be here?''

''Lieutenant Tynan, yes.''

''We expected someone a little older than you.''

Tynan ignored that and moved to the chair. He sat
down, stared into each of the faces, and then said, ''I'm
afraid I have no idea what this is all about.''

The man who had spoken slipped into his chair and
opened a leather binder. Without bothering to introduce
any of the people in the room, he said, ''Everything

discussed in this room is restricted. I don't want to hear any of it on the evening news tonight. That clear?''

When everyone had nodded, the man said, ''Then we'll begin.'' He reached under the table and the lights dimmed as the screen slipped quietly from the ceiling. From a place hidden in the wall, a slide projector snapped on and a map of Central America appeared.

''For the benefit of those of you who do not know what is happening''—he looked pointedly at Tynan—''I'll provide a bit of background.''

For the next five minutes he went over everything that was known about the sudden disappearance of the scientific expedition in Honduras. It was surprisingly little. When he finished, the projector turned off and the screen began its climb into the ceiling.

''Are there any questions?'' he asked with the confidence of a man who expected none.

Tynan raised a hand and asked, ''Did the radio room record the conversation and, if so, can we get a copy of that tape?''

''You think that's important?'' asked one of the men.

Tynan looked at him and said, ''Can't tell without hearing the tape, if it exists. It would seem to me, however, that such a tape might provide some clues in the background noise.''

The leader of the group pointed to one of the other men and said, ''I want you to check it out.''

The man nodded and pulled a pen from his pocket to make a note.

''No, I want you to check it out now. Get on the phone and see what you can learn.''

The man stood and said, ''Yes, sir.'' He left the room quickly.

Tynan watched him go and then said, ''This would be easier if I knew who was involved in this.''

''Lieutenant, you don't have to know who we are. Our

mission right now is to determine whether your particular field of expertise will be of benefit or not.''

"Then maybe I should wait elsewhere while you determine the answer.''

The man pulled a sheet of paper from his leather folder and slid it across the table. "You are here under orders and you will stay here until I decide that you will leave.''

Tynan dragged the paper close and spun it around so that he could read it. He glanced up and asked, "Are you Douglas Moffit?''

"Yes.''

"Do you have some identification?''

"Lieutenant, I am not in the habit of identifying myself to every junior level employee who shows up here.''

"Yes, sir,'' said Tynan. "This says that I'm to report to Douglas Moffit and I can't follow those instructions unless I know who everyone is.''

Moffit stared at Tynan for ten seconds and then reached into the inside pocket of his suit. He pulled his wallet out and said, "I assume that my driver's license will be sufficient.''

Under normal circumstances, a driver's license *wouldn't* be sufficient. There were too many ways for a driver's license to be faked, but Tynan knew that the man had to be who he said he was. He examined the license carefully, thinking that he should quiz the man about it, but decided he was already being enough of an asshole. He flipped it back to Moffit.

"Now,'' Moffit said, "if there are no other questions, we can get back to the important aspects of this meeting.'' He glanced around the room.

No one looked back at him. They kept their eyes on the floor or on the table. The silence lengthened uncomfortably until the door opened.

As the man entered, he said, "They did make a tape of the radio transmission. They said that so much information is transmitted during those messages, that they have to make a tape. Then, afterward, everyone can listen to it and make suggestions about procedure.''

''Did you think to ask for a copy of the tape?'' asked Moffit.

''I did you one better. I asked them to play it into the phone while we recorded it here. Ten more minutes and we should be able to listen to it.''

Moffit rocked back in his chair, a look of mock surprise on his face. ''What? You took the initiative to do that? I'm stunned.''

The man ignored that as he slipped into his seat.

''Anyone have any questions that he or she wants to ask while we're waiting?''

Tynan had a dozen that he wanted to ask, but decided to sit quietly until he could learn something more of what was happening. He studied the people in the room with him and wondered if any of them ever got out of Washington. None of them looked as if they ever walked in the sun. They all seemed to buy their clothes in the same store, off the same rack, and they all seemed to go to the same barber or hairstylist. About the only real difference among them was eye color. Idly, Tynan wondered what the preferred eye color for someone in their line of work would be.

The door opened again and a young man entered carrying a tape recorder. Without speaking, he set it in the center of the table, strung out the cord and then crawled along the wall until he found an outlet. Finally he stood and moved to his machine. One hand on the switch, he said, ''The quality of the recording isn't the best. We can have a better copy flown in if you want.''

''Just get on with it,'' snapped Moffit.

''Yes, sir.'' The man turned on the recorder and said, ''The first few seconds will be a high pitched buzz. Then we get into the good stuff.''

Tynan watched the reels of the recorder spin for a moment, then closed his eyes to concentrate on the sound.

It was a poor quality recording, but he could understand enough of it. Routine stuff from an expedition of scientists. Radio procedure was weak or nonexistent.

All that changed suddenly. There was a whirring noise that sounded almost like a mortar round dropping in, but there was no accompanying explosion. Shouts of confusion that became unintelligible. A few shots and a few screams. Finally there was a screeching howl that drowned out all sound. Then that snapped off suddenly, sounding as if someone had shut down the radio.

When the tape ended, Moffit asked, "Anyone have any ideas?"

"We need to get someone in there to look around," said one of the women.

Moffit turned to stare at Tynan. "Lieutenant, I think you can figure out who is going to go in and look around. You have any comments?"

"Other than it sounds as if the party was attacked, no."

"I was hoping for something a little more defined," said Moffit. "A little more detail."

"Yes," agreed Tynan, "that would be nice. Except that there's nothing I can tell you. Sounded like incoming mortars but without the explosions. A few shots from a small-caliber weapon and screams of panic. That's all I can pick up from the tape."

"What would be your next move, Lieutenant," asked Moffit, "if you were to make one?"

"An interview with the people at the university about the nature of the expedition. And since this took place outside the United States, I would register a protest with the Honduran government."

"Protesting what?" asked one of the men.

"How about the lack of information about the expedition?" said Tynan. "The Honduran government could put people into the field to look at the campsite. That might tell us something."

"Lieutenant, you haven't thought this through. We can't

tell the Honduran government that we know what has happened. If they had any idea that we were running recon over their territory, they'd protest to the United Nations.''

"Fine," said Tynan, "don't tell them how much you know. Still, there's no reason you can't tell them that the expedition is in trouble."

Now Moffit was quiet. He looked at the others and said, "Well, our feeling is that we'd prefer not to rely on a foreign government. We'd rather handle it on our own. That tends to limit our response."

"I don't understand that," said Tynan. "A couple of helos, maybe off a carrier in the region, and you've got your answer."

"Again, Lieutenant, there are things about this that you don't know. There are very good reasons why we can't engage in aerial surveillance. And the choppers wouldn't be able to land . . ."

"Why the hell not?"

"Political reasons," said Moffit. "We must make our recon on the sly, as it were."

"But if time is that important, you're wasting a great deal of it," said Tynan.

"The feeling," said Moffit pointedly, "is that a couple of days, one way or the other, is not going to alter the facts of the situation. We can move in without the Honduran government knowing a thing about it. That's the way it's going to be. Now, are there any other questions?"

Tynan lifted his hand and said, "So we all rush to Washington so that we can take our time getting to Honduras?"

Moffit closed his leather folder and then studied his group. "I don't see where further discussion of this situation is going to lead us anywhere. We have all the information available to us now."

He waited and then said, "Lieutenant Tynan, you will

travel to the university and see if there is anything else to be ascertained there. Once that is completed, you will make arrangements to travel to Honduras for the purpose of locating the expedition.''

"Wait!'' said Tynan. "I'm to do this by myself?''

"A team is being assembled for you. Fellow SEALS, I believe. A list was provided by your Navy. They will meet you in Honduras.''

"No,'' said Tynan.

"Sir?'' said Moffit, surprised. "What do you mean by no? No is not an acceptable response.''

"I don't want to travel into this environment with men I don't know and haven't worked with.''

"They've all had the same training that you've had and are being screened by your own people.''

Tynan wanted to tell the man that it meant nothing. In a combat environment, you wanted men you knew and trusted. Men whose reactions were automatic. Men you had seen under stress. But he knew that the buttoned-down bureaucrat would not, could not, understand the subtlety of a combat situation; and although this wasn't a combat situation, the stresses would be the same, if he'd read the briefing correctly. But if Tynan refused without good reason, Moffit would just trot out the orders and tell Tynan that there was no choice in the matter.

To Moffit, he said, "I can think of a number of logistical problems that would have to be worked out before we could even think of deploying.''

"Diplomatic pouches and couriers cover a multitude of sins,'' said Moffit. "You let my office know what you want and we'll see that it arrives.''

Tynan decided to try a different approach. "I'm afraid I don't have the expertise to follow up on this. I know nothing of the region or the people.''

"Intelligence briefings can be arranged quickly. I know that someone on your end is screening the team to make sure that all the needs are filled.''

Tynan sat quietly for a moment, his mind racing. He tried to think of reasons to refuse the mission, but each time he thought of something, he could already hear the answer. Weapons? Smuggled in by diplomatic pouch if necessary. Lack of knowledge of the region? Someone else would have it. Equipment? Tell me what you want and we'll get it for you. Taking too much time to put it together? Then you'd better hurry.

And in the end he would have to go anyway. Moffit was sitting there, his fingers drumming on the sheet of paper that contained his orders, as if to prove that he, Moffit, could make Tynan do anything he wanted him to. The orders were the killer. Someone in State had called someone at the Pentagon and the orders were cut. No questions about it. ("Oh, if you need something in the future, don't hesitate to call.") Washington establishment working at its finest. I'll help you now if you'll help me later, and it worked even better for the Navy because no one in Washington had to do a thing except make a few phone calls.

There was absolutely no way that Tynan could get out of it. To refuse would be the same as refusing an order in the Navy. It would be the end of his career.

"All right," Tynan said reluctantly. "I'll check this out, though I would think that others would be more qualified to pursue it."

"You let me worry about that," said Moffit. "Your driver will be waiting to take you back to National Airport. Tickets will be waiting at the Delta desk and arrangements have been made at the other end."

Tynan stood and said, "In that case, I imagine I had better get going."

"And check in with my office," warned Moffit.

Within three hours, Tynan was in another city, riding in a station wagon assigned to the university, driven by Stephanie King. Her hair was long in the current fashion, hanging down her back and brushed toward her eyes in bangs.

She wore faded blue jeans and a rough, cotton shirt. Tynan assumed she was a student.

She hadn't said much as she picked him up at the airport. On the drive into the university, she kept her mouth shut, her lips a thin, bloodless line. She stared straight ahead, her knuckles white on the wheel.

Tynan wasn't sure why she was angry but after the first few abortive attempts at conversation, he'd decided to relax until he learned more. It was obvious that she knew something and she wasn't about to share it with him.

The university was alive with students and giant trees. The buildings, most of them looking as if they had been erected around the turn of the century, dominated the center of the city. A mist of rain dampened everything and the low-hanging clouds added to the somber mood.

They parked in the faculty lot. King was out of the car and walking up the walk without a word almost before Tynan could open his door. Tynan followed quickly, watched her open a door and disappear inside. He caught her as she climbed the steps toward the second floor.

"What's the deal here?" he asked.

She stopped at the top of the steps and looked down at him. "The deal is that we don't need interference from the federal government. It's a problem that we could handle on our own without some hotshot from Washington blowing in here to show us how to do everything."

Tynan felt a smile spread across his face and then he began to laugh. "Is that what this is about? You resent me because I'm the Washington hotshot?"

She didn't answer; simply turned and continued up the stairs and along the hallway. Tynan had to hurry to catch her again.

She opened a door and then stepped back. Tynan hesitated and then entered. He saw a man sitting behind a massive desk adrift with papers and folders. There was a table in front of the desk, also loaded with papers; and the walls were ringed with bookcases filled with thousands of volumes. There was a single window behind the desk.

The man stood and came forward with his hand out. "I'm Thomas."

"Tynan."

"Well, Mr. Tynan, I know that you've been briefed on our problem. I'm afraid that there's nothing new we can add to what you already know." He stopped talking, stared, and then added, "Please have a seat. I'm afraid I've gotten ahead of myself."

Tynan pulled a chair away from the table and sat down as Thomas moved to the door. He pushed it open and said, "Stevie, I think we want you in on this, too."

King shrugged and entered, taking a chair opposite of Tynan. Thomas waved a hand and said, "You've met Dr. King."

Tynan grinned and said, "Not really. She provided a ride from the airport."

"Oh. I think I understand now," said Thomas, nodding. "She tends to take things personally, but she gets over them quickly." He stepped to his chair behind his desk and dropped into it. "Now that we're all here, I guess we can get started."

"Started at what?" asked Tynan.

"Planning the trip. Dr. King will be our representative on it."

Tynan laughed once, a sound without humor. "Now, wait a damn minute."

"I told you that he wouldn't listen to that," snapped King.

"Be patient," said Thomas. "Mr. Tynan, I don't think that you understand. We have to have a representative on the expedition and Dr. King is the most qualified."

"Qualified for what?"

"To evaluate the data," she snapped. "To understand the find and to determine the importance of it."

Tynan shook his head. "I thought that this was a recon

to discover your last expedition. I didn't sign on to baby-sit a second expedition."

"I don't think you understand, Mr. Tynan. You were asked here so that we could mount the second attempt. One of the goals—the primary goal—is to determine the fate of our first group, but we must also complete the goals of the first expedition."

"People have been talking around this expedition all day and no one seems to know what it was all about," said Tynan.

"Well, the exact nature of it is a little abstract, I'm afraid. We're investigating some information that we've just come into possession of. The exact nature of the expedition isn't that important now."

"If I'm going to have to complete the goals of the first mission, then I've got to know what they are."

"Well, maybe I spoke a little too quickly. All you really must do is determine the fate of the first expedition. Once that is done, you'll be free to return to your base."

Tynan rubbed his face and then looked at King. She stared stonily at the window to her left. There was something else going on here that Tynan didn't understand. There was something he wasn't being told, and past experience had shown that everytime that happened, he found himself holding the short end of the stick.

Thomas leaned forward, both elbows on his desk, his hands clasped under his nose. He was waiting for Tynan to pick up the ball and run with it.

"What preparations have you people made?" Tynan finally asked when he was sure that neither of them was going to elaborate on the first expedition.

"Full gear is waiting to be loaded on the truck to take to the airport. Maps, food, water, and radios have all been checked and readied."

Now Tynan looked at King. "You've been in the jungle before?"

"I've been out camping a few times."

"I'm not talking about a trip into the forests here, where help is only a mile or so away. I'm not talking about a benign forest filled with furry creatures. I'm talking about a jungle with poisonous snakes and poisonous plants, where help is days away."

"I'm aware of the problem," she said icily.

"Weapons?" said Tynan. "Did you make provisions for carrying weapons?"

"We do not have the proper clearances, nor the experience to deal with weapons."

"Uh-huh," said Tynan. "I take it that you've listened to that tape."

"Yes."

"Then you know that whatever happened to those people was not the result of a natural disaster in the jungle. They were attacked by someone or something, and now you intend to enter that same environment without taking a single weapon for your own protection."

Now it was Thomas who smiled. "I was assured that your special training included some knowledge of firearms and weapons. I have left that area alone, hoping that you would be in a position to take care of it."

Tynan rocked back in his chair and took a deep breath. He could almost taste the age of the room. He could almost hear the learned discussions that had taken place in it: discussions about the true nature of the human race; how that definition had been changed throughout history; arguments about the fossil record and if the new bit of evidence changed the known path of evolutionary thinking; abstract discussions about life on the Serengeti Plain a million years ago.

"Dr. Thomas, it would be better if I went in without your people. Let me check out the situation, and then you can make plans for another expedition so I won't accidentally find out what it was all about. But you can do that after we learn the fate of the first."

"Mr. Tynan, I'm afraid that the university doesn't have the resources to underwrite two more expeditions. We must combine the two."

"This is not a walk in the park. It's going to be a dangerous operation."

"Yes, well, the quest for knowledge often follows the dangerous path. If we wait until all danger is removed, the progress of the human race will come to a standstill. Nothing is certain in this life. No, the danger and the hazards might be great, but it is a chance that we must take."

Tynan turned his attention to the woman. "You prepared to take this risk?"

"I can handle anything that you can," she said.

Tynan shook his head and realized that it was all moving too fast. Too many other people were making decisions that they weren't qualified to make. The intelligent thing to do was sit back and let the Hondurans send in a team. Wait for the results. He could understand the university people wanting to act immediately. It was the same reaction that he would have in a similar circumstance. But that didn't mean they should fly off half-cocked, trying to lose more people. Caution and intelligence should dictate the response.

"Why don't you all wait a week? Give me a chance to get in there and see if I can learn anything more."

"I want my people there when you get to the site," said Thomas. "They might be able to determine something that you or your people would overlook. No matter what you say, this is still a scientific expedition."

Tynan looked at the woman again. He had nothing against her. He just didn't believe a woman raised in the civilized environment of the United States could understand the hardships of the jungle without some kind of training. He knew that she was overestimating her ability and underestimating the danger of the jungle.

"I don't suppose that there is any way to talk you out of this," he said.

Thomas shook his head. "Not really."

"Then I guess we'd better get going."

"I guess you better," said Thomas.

4

The flight from the local airport to Tegucigalpa was a long and tedious one. The seats in the rear of the commercial airliner had been jammed together, not allowing much in either shoulder- or leg-room, but letting the airline cram as many people in the tiny fuselage as possible.

Once they were airborne, the flight attendants moved through the cabin handing out soft drinks and beer and wine, and taking orders and money for mixed drinks. Tynan had taken a beer and then waited as King ordered a Coke. Until that moment, she had kept her nose buried in a text about the high civilizations of Mesoamerica.

When she looked up to accept the Coke from the attendant, Tynan said, "If we're going to work together, we're going to have to talk."

She sipped her Coke and then looked at Tynan. Her face softened and she said, "I suppose so."

"There is something that has been bothering me since I got here. No one has answered the question and I don't know whether it's because they've been avoiding it on purpose or if it's because no one knows."

She lowered her tray table and set both her book and the Coke on it. "What is it you want to know?"

Tynan grinned and asked, "Just what in the hell were those people doing in the Honduran jungle?"

King drank some more Coke and then pensively swirled her glass around, letting the ice rattle. Finally she shrugged, as if she had just made up her mind about something. "This is off the record," she cautioned, and then plunged on. "They were searching for, trying to verify, some interesting information that we had."

"Uh-huh," said Tynan. "That tells me nothing."

"Are you at all familiar with the Mayan culture?" she asked suddenly, as if to change the subject.

"I know that it was a fairly advanced civilization that built some amazing cities in Mexico and Central America and that it disappeared overnight."

"Not exactly overnight, but they did disappear. No one knows exactly why they packed up and moved, or even exactly where they went. Theories abound: Water ran out and they had to move. Soil was depleted forcing a migration. Invasion or civil war. Maybe disease. There's even a new idea suggesting that the people in the city, now outside the food-producing activities, had too much leisure time. Decay from within. No one knows for sure."

"Just as I said."

She nodded. Her voice had taken on a warmth that it had been lacking. Suddenly she was no longer in the rear of an airplane flying south, but standing in front of a graduate seminar, lecturing. The information she had was no longer something to be guarded. It was something to be shared so that the whole academic world would be able to study it.

"Then, suddenly, we have information of a lost Mayan city. A city in the jungle that has never been seen by white men and women. A secret, sacred place of the Mayans."

"Of course," said Tynan.

She shifted around so that she could look at him. Her eyes were bright with excitement. "I know what you're thinking. It's what each of us thought when we first heard the news. 'Another story of a lost city.' The only thing missing were the tales of wealth beyond all imagination.

Gold and silver and jade that would require an army to move. But we've got proof. Not of the gold, but of the city.''

''Someone give you a map?'' asked Tynan sarcastically, immediately regretting it. The whole thing sounded far-fetched, but at least she was talking to him and that was progress.

But she choose to ignore his flip remark. She glanced around like a fugitive looking for the law. When she saw that no one was interested in her conversation, she said, ''Yes. That's exactly what we've got. A map, of sorts.''

''Come on,'' said Tynan. ''That's the oldest dodge in the world.''

''Yes, unless you know the source of your map.''

''Source?''

''We knew this one was good. We knew the map they provided showed exactly where the city was. Oh, you wouldn't recognize it as a city unless you knew what to look for, but we did, and we found it.''

Tynan leaned closer, suddenly aware of King as a woman. There was a fragrance drifting from her that was exciting. Tynan didn't want to notice it. Not after her attitude during the drive to the college and in the anthro office. She was good-looking, intelligent, and he wanted to keep the woman as distant as he would the men of his unit, assigned to what could become a combat mission.

''That doesn't make sense,'' he said.

''No, of course not,'' she said. ''Let me say this first: we'd heard the rumors of the city for years. South and Central America are alive with rumors of lost cities. Some of them have turned out to be true. It wasn't until the turn of the century that Machu Picchu was found.''

''I understand that.''

''And it's not possible to chase down each and every rumor. But then came the space age. Satellites flying all over the globe, taking pictures from deep space that are transmitted to Earth. Pictures of every square inch of ground. Through connections, we were able to obtain copies of the pictures of Honduras, and by studying them carefully, we found the lost city. A place where the jungle thins and the temperature signatures suggest rock or stone formations close to the surface where stone formations shouldn't be."

"So you found a huge meteor fall."

She sat back and stared. "That's very good. Most people wouldn't have thought of it."

"I try."

"Using the material we had at hand, we determined that the stone formations were too regular to be attributed to a meteor fall. In other words, it wasn't a random pattern as you'd have in nature, but something that had been built by human hands."

"So, on the basis of this, you sent your people into the jungle."

"No," she said. "We had other evidence, too. Archaeological evidence. Pots of Mayan origin in the area. Artifacts brought out of the jungle. Stories coming out of the jungle. There is *some*thing there. We know that. We just don't know what it is."

"So you just sent your people in?"

"Why not? This is the twentieth century. Exploration of the jungle isn't all that hazardous anymore. Not with radios and helicopters and airplanes."

"I'll have to concede you that one."

She pulled out a book containing a rough map of the region. "You see? There are ruins all through the area. Mayan and Aztec and Toltec and even some Olmec. Some aren't large, only a temple on a hill of stone. Others are very elaborate. Any new find in the area, if untouched since the Mayans left it, would be the biggest news in the world of archaeology since King Tut."

"I'm suitably impressed," Tynan said.

She lowered her voice again and added, "And whoever

made the find, regardless of who'd done the work at the university, would have her ticket filled.''

"I understand." And he did. It had nothing to do with danger or the missing people. It had to do with building careers and sealing a place in history.

"When we arrive," she cautioned, "you can't spread the word about this lost city. If others learn how close we are, they'll try to beat us to the city."

"But we're not going to the city," Tynan reminded her. "We're looking for your friends."

"Of course," she said, looking away. "That's the number-one priority. We've got to find out what happened to all those people." She didn't say anything more, but she planned to drag them on, deeper into the jungle, where the lost city lay hidden from the world.

The landing at Tegucigalpa was uneventful. They disembarked, checked through Customs and then headed for the American Embassy, where Tynan hoped to learn something about the men he was to meet. He had thought they were already in the country, flown in the night before, but that turned out to be wrong. They would be arriving by boat the next evening. And they would be carrying the equipment and weapons Tynan believed necessary for the mission.

Tynan sat in the naval attaché's office, King next to him, and watched as the naval officer searched through the cables and messages that he had received the day before. He kept glancing at King, and Tynan didn't know if he was interested in her, or if he was irritated that she had followed them into the office without being asked.

Commander Richard Cook pulled a map from the folder and studied it silently. Holding on to it, he stared at King.

"Commander," said Tynan, "she's on this all the way. Anything you can tell me, you can tell her."

"Lieutenant, this is not exactly information that should be handed out to the civilian world."

King swung and looked at him. "Lieutenant? You're one of them?"

"If you mean an officer in the military, yes."

"Shit," she said in a single bark. She turned away from him, her eyes on the floor.

"Did I let something out of the bag?" asked Cook.

"No," said Tynan. "I probably should have made it clear from the beginning but it just never came up."

"Oh no," snapped King. "You let Dr. Thomas call you 'mister' a dozen times and never corrected him."

Tynan rubbed his eye and then said, "Dr. Thomas was fully cognizant of my status. I assumed that he mentioned it to those of you who had to know."

King stood and stepped to the door. "I think it's time that we sever this relationship. I can't work with the hypocrisy and the deception."

"Where are you going?" asked Tynan.

She stood with one hand on the doorknob. "Out. I'll arrange my own transportation into the field. I'll find my own guides."

"I'm afraid we can't have that," said Cook.

"Oh, really?" said King. "Well, I'm not one of your military flunkies. I don't take orders from you. There isn't a thing you can do to stop me."

Cook reached out and touched the phone on the corner of his desk. "That's where you're wrong. We're not in the United States now. Outside the walls of this embassy is a foreign country, where they may not believe in the individual rights we have in the United States. One phone call and you'll find out just how limited your movements can be."

"Are you threatening me?"

"Exactly." Cook grinned and waved at the vacated seat. "Why not sit down and we'll all cooperate?"

"What in the hell is going on out there that you people find so fascinating?"

Cook shrugged. "There's nothing out there of interest to

us. But we have the report that American citizens were attacked by something and we want to find out what. We want to protect our citizens. That's our job.''

Still King hadn't moved.

"It's nothing more sinister than that, Ms. King, I assure you.''

"*Dr*. King.''

"Certainly. Why don't you have a seat and we'll get on with this.''

King returned to the seat but didn't look happy. Cook continued the briefing, using the map. Two four-wheel-drive vehicles were going to be provided. They were to drive south out of Tegucigalpa along the only major road until they reached the swamp areas near the western coast. At San Lorenzo they were to turn to the east, staying with the road until they reached the northern edge of Gulfo de Fonseca. The rest of the team would arrive by rubber boat as soon as they received the all-clear signal.

"And that will be?'' asked Tynan.

"A flashing light. Two long, one short, two long. Wait, and then repeat it.''

"Christ,'' sneered King. "Sounds like something from a spy movie.''

"How far is it to the rendezvous point?'' asked Tynan.

"No more than sixty miles. Road is good the whole way and it's only at the very end that you'll want to pull off it. The drive, barring an earthquake or the end of life as we know it, shouldn't take more than two hours.''

Tynan moved forward so he could study the map. He glanced at King, who sat facing away from them, staring at the bookcases to her left.

He turned his attention back to the map and said, "Seems simple enough.''

"It is. Once you've picked up the rest of your team, you'll have to study the maps to see what the best route into the boondocks is. I think you'll be able to drive within fifteen or twenty miles of the site.''

Again Tynan looked at King, but she seemed completely uninterested. He asked, "You know where the expedition was?"

Cook touched the map. "Around here. Once you're into the area, I think you'll be able to locate it quickly."

"Fly overs?"

"Nothing visible on any of the photos, including the pictures taken by our recon aircraft, but that doesn't mean much. The jungle is fairly thick there."

Tynan finally pushed the map away and asked, "Why haven't you put helos into the field to check all this out?"

Cook looked from King to Tynan and said, "My orders were to keep this under wraps. Helicopter flights in and out would call attention to the situation."

Tynan shook his head and wondered about that. Again, everyone wanted to rush, rush, rush, but no one wanted to make waves.

Cook continued the briefing, occasionally looking at King, who seemed to have no interest in anything that was going on around her. He then sat down again and asked, "Any questions?"

There was nothing that Tynan could think of. He turned to King. "Doctor?"

"No."

"All right," Cook said. "I'll be here or within a phone call of here. Someone will always be able to reach me within minutes, so if you need anything, you get in touch."

"The vehicles?" said Tynan.

"Will be ready first thing in the morning. Until then, we'll give you a car. Marks you as an American and someone with connections at the embassy, but I don't think that's a problem."

With that, both King and Tynan left Cook's office. They walked down the hallway to the elevator. Neither spoke as they waited and neither spoke as they walked out of the embassy. A Marine led them to the car and handed

Tynan the keys. The Marine made him sign for it, then left.

"Is there anything you want to do now?" Tynan asked as he got in.

The thawing that had begun on the plane was now completely reversed. She answered his question as quickly and tersely as possible: "I just want to get to the hotel."

Tynan sat quietly for a moment, staring through the windshield. Finally, he put the key in the ignition and started the car. "Fine."

The room Tynan was given looked like nearly every other hotel room he had ever had. This hotel, affiliated with a major American chain, differed from those hotels only in location. Everything about it, including the black-and-white television on a stand near the dresser, was American. A window air conditioner held the humidity and heat at bay.

Tynan dropped to the single bed, laced his fingers behind his head, and stared at the ceiling. He tried to concentrate on the mission at hand, but found he just couldn't take it seriously. Even after hearing the tape in Washington, he wasn't impressed with it. There was nothing to worry about. The radio had failed and, during that failure, had produced some very unusual broadcasts. That was all there was to it. This was just going to be a walk in the Honduran jungle. He couldn't see how anything in the jungle in Honduras would present a danger that he, along with four or five other men trained as SEALS, couldn't handle. Scientists and graduate students might be overwhelmed by the unusual, but certainly not highly trained Navy SEALS.

The phone sitting on the nightstand beeped at him. He rolled over and lifted it. He was surprised when King identified herself and asked if he wanted to eat dinner with her. He agreed and then sat up, grinning at the phone as he hung up.

Obviously, she had called her people in the States and been told to cooperate with Tynan. Someone might have told her that the military people could be used, if she did nothing to alienate them. At any rate, she was going to have to cooperate. She wouldn't have changed her mind without someone ordering her to change it.

Tynan changed into trousers and a light blue shirt. He thought about a tie, but decided that in the tropics, even inside an air-conditioned hotel, it was a useless piece of apparel. In fact, he couldn't see the point of a tie at all. At the door, he stopped and scanned the room, noticing where everything was. He snapped off the lights and headed for the elevator.

King was in the lobby waiting for him. She wore a light dress that was cut low. She had a light jacket over her arm. She smiled as she came toward him.

"We can eat here or go out," she said.

Tynan looked across the expanse of the lobby floor. Marble and dark carpet. High-backed chairs and couches. A few tables. And the registration desk that dominated one wall. To one side was a recessed door with a stained-glass window.

"In there would be fine," said Tynan.

King turned and headed for the door, she waited for Tynan to open it, and then entered. The interior was dark. Mahogany paneling covered the walls and there were candles on each of the tables, but that did little to chase the gloom. There were only a few people in the restaurant since it was early to be eating in Latin American.

King found a table away from the bar, the front door, and the kitchen. She sat down without waiting for Tynan to pull out her chair. She propped both elbows on the table and leaned forward, deepening her cleavage.

"Now, Lieutenant, tell me about yourself."

Tynan glanced at her breasts and then at her eyes. He shrugged and said, "What in the hell happened?"

"What do you mean?"

"An hour ago you were so angry that you wouldn't talk. Now you're down here trying your hardest to be nice."

"So I changed my mind."

"Un-huh," said Tynan. "The question is why did you change your mind."

"I'm a woman and that gives me the right."

"You're a scientist," said Tynan, "and a scientist works from facts."

Finally she sat back and let her eyes fall. "Okay. I realized that if we're to accomplish our goals, I'll need to cooperate with you. I thought of this as an opportunity for a peace treaty."

Now Tynan smiled. "Then, why didn't you just say so? There was no reason to be sneaky about it."

"Okay," she said, holding a hand across the table. "Peace?"

Tynan shook her hand. "Peace."

They ordered and then ate their meal slowly. They talked about the Navy, the disappearances, and finally about the Mayans and the Olmecs. King mentioned that the majority of the finds were in Mexico, south of the area of influence of the Aztecs. There were a few ancient sites in Guatemala. Nothing other than Copán had been found in this area until they had made their discovery.

"It's what made the expedition worthwhile. It might have provided a clue about the collapse of the Mayan civilization."

"But first, we have another mystery to solve," said Tynan. "What happened to the expedition?"

"There is that," she said. "You have any ideas?"

Tynan rubbed his chin, took a drink from his glass of water, and said, "My training is not in the investigation of mysteries, though I've been involved in a couple of cases somewhat similar. I've learned not to speculate until I've had a chance to review the evidence. I'll wait until we arrive on site."

She smiled then and said, "I meant, do you have any

ideas for tonight? We've got the whole evening together and I'm not ready for Spanish-language television.''

"I just figured on eating dinner and drinking as much as I could. Water, that is. Before a mission into the jungle, it's a good idea to eat and drink as much as possible. You can live a long time off the energy."

"Now, that certainly is an entertaining idea," she said. She leaned forward slowly. The fabric of her blouse pulled apart slightly, revealing her cleavage. She smiled broadly, and then suddenly sat back.

"I'm sorry," she said.

"Sorry?"

"Yes. I don't know what I was thinking. Suddenly I had the urge to seduce you. I don't know why. Maybe because there is really nothing else to do tonight, or maybe I thought you'd help me if I needed it." She shrugged.

"I don't follow."

"No reason you should. There was a moment there that I wanted to go to bed with you . . . Let's forget the whole thing."

Tynan stared at her and then dropped his eyes. He thought of a dozen things to say and decided against them all. Her confusion gave him the answer to one question. Her hostile attitude wasn't completely the result of Tynan's military connection. Part of it was because she found herself liking him, even though he was a military officer.

The best thing he could do was ignore the conflicting signals she was giving off. Let her sort through the problem with no pressure from him. Besides, he wasn't sure that he wanted to get involved with her. More important, he certainly didn't want to get involved before they hit the field.

So he turned his attention to his meal and let the conversation die. The conversational path was strewn with too many land mines. After the mission, that was a different story. But before? No way.

They finished their meal quickly and quietly. When the

check came, King reached for it. "The university said that I should pick up a few of the expenses on this."

"I never argue with free food," Tynan said.

They left the restaurant together and walked to the elevators. Tynan escorted King to her room and then left when she got the key in the lock. He thought about a good-night kiss, but knew it could lead to problems. Problems he didn't want to face. He beat a hasty retreat, calling "Good night" as he headed for the elevators.

Upstairs, he entered his own room and was suddenly alert. There was something wrong, though he couldn't put his finger on it. He stood with his back to the door, his eyes scanning.

It was the curtains. He had pulled them, shutting out the night lights of the city. Now they stood open. He glanced at the bed but it hadn't been turned down. That meant someone other than the maid had been in the room.

He slipped along the wall until he stood close to the bed. From there, he could see into the bathroom, but it was empty. Who ever had been in the room was gone now. Tynan reached to the right and touched the light switch.

Everything was where he'd left it. He moved to the suitcase and opened it. There were subtle changes there— the clothes not exactly as he'd left them, but close. He reached up under them and found the four fifty-dollar bills that he'd put there.

So it hadn't been a thief. A clever thief would have taken two so that Tynan would think he'd spent the other two sometime and forgotten. But a really smart man, searching Tynan's room, would have taken them all, figuring that if Tynan noticed something, he'd assume a thief. This guy had outsmarted himself.

Tynan made sure that he was alone and then sat on the bed. It could be a coincidence. It could have been the maid on some last-minute cleaning campaign. It could have been a sloppy thief who failed to find the money and who was looking for a camera. Or it could have been someone interested in learning what Tynan was doing in Tegucigalpa.

The question was, did it matter? In the morning, he would return to the embassy, pick up the vehicles, and head south. Someone in his hotel room would become unimportant. Besides, there was nothing going on that made the search important. His mission wasn't secret. The Honduran government, the American government, and two thousand other people knew exactly what he was doing.

He thought about calling King to warn her, but decided that the searchers wouldn't return while they were in the room. If she hadn't discovered that her room had been searched, there was no reason to alarm her.

It all might be the result of the embassy car they had used. Everyone knew they were from the American Embassy. It could be someone looking for information about them.

Or it all could be his imagination. It looked as if someone had gone through his room, but they had stolen nothing and there had been nothing for them to find. The best course of action seemed to be to ignore the situation.

He wished now that he had insisted on a weapon. The embassy guards could have let him have a pistol for the evening. Just something, in case. Tomorrow, the men coming in would have quite a few weapons, but tonight he had nothing other than a folding knife with a three-inch blade.

He sat down on the bed and realized that he had the perfect excuse to call her. He could go down to her room and make a production out of searching it. Maybe suggest that they spend the night together for mutual safety. It was a tailor-made dodge.

But then again, he just wasn't ready for the entanglements. And since the intruder had been careful not to disturb his clothes, seabag, and papers, he doubted there was any danger. Calling attention to it might prove more dangerous than ignoring it.

There was nothing that he could do about it. He locked the door, used the chain, and then slipped a chair up under the knob. Someone determined could get in, but they would make enough noise to wake the dead and that was all that Tynan wanted. A little warning.

5

Tynan was up with the sun. He changed into fatigues that had no insignia on them. Dark green clothes, jungle boots, and a boonie hat to keep the sun out of his eyes. He had web gear, but wouldn't need it until later. He didn't even fill the canteens, because he could do that at the embassy.

He packed everything else into his seabag and hauled it downstairs. He checked out of the hotel and then sat in the lobby waiting for King to appear. She came down about an hour later, also ready to begin the expedition.

Tynan had to laugh when he saw her. If there was a stereotype of the jungle huntress, she was it. A khaki bush jacket with huge loops on the breast for the large-caliber cartridges that would bring down an elephant. She wore a knee-length khaki skirt and tan knee socks. All she needed was a pith helmet to complete the costume. When she set one on the registration desk, Tynan burst out laughing.

Once she had paid for her room, she moved toward Tynan and asked, "You ready?"

Tynan got up, shouldered his seabag, and headed toward the door. They got into the car and drove to the embassy. Cook was waiting for them and took them back out to where the four-wheel drive vehicles waited. They were little more than glorified jeeps, both painted a bright red with white trim.

"Makes aerial search for them easier," explained Cook. "They stand out like beacons."

Tynan opened the rear of one and tossed his seabag in the back. He then walked around to the front, opened the driver's door and looked inside. He noticed the lever that shifted the vehicle from two-wheel to four-wheel drive.

"Anything about that I should know?"

"Just don't try to make the change with the transmission engaged or while moving."

"I know better than that."

Cook turned to King. "Can you drive a stick shift?"

She touched a hand to her pith helmet as if holding it on in a high wind. "I'm not completely helpless. Of course I can drive a stick shift."

Again Cook showed them the map. Tynan said, "Why don't you take the lead, Stevie? You can find this San Lorenzo. If we get separated for any reason, stop where the road loops to the west. I'll meet you there."

"And why would we get separated?"

"Who knows? It's just best to have a plan in case that happens. You lead and I'll bring up the rear."

She shrugged and nodded.

Cook folded the map and said, "Radios in the back have plenty of range. You get into trouble, give us a shout. In any case, try to make a radio check at six every evening."

"You know," said Tynan, "for a great expedition into the jungle, this seems to be a fairly loosely planned activity. It's not like driving to Grandma's house for Sunday lunch."

"By the same token," said Cook, "it's not like you're embarking into the great uncharted regions of Africa. We can get help to you within an hour with helicopters."

"There is that," said Tynan. "The only thing I want to do is make sure that we've got enough water."

Cook pointed to the rear of the jeep. "Couple of containers in there with fifteen, twenty gallons. You can fill your canteens over there.'' He pointed to the right, where there were lush, tropical plantings in stark contrast to the white of the embassy building: towering green palms, ferns with delicate leaves, and bushes with huge orange and pink blossoms.

Tynan worked his way into the bush and found a spicket. He used it to fill his canteens and then carried them back to the jeep.

''Now,'' said Cook, ''the natives are friendly, especially in the boonies. They all like Americans, so if you get into trouble, don't feel afraid of approaching people. About the only anti-American sentiment is in the major urban centers, and even then, it's something that's generated for the TV cameras.''

''Got it,'' said Tynan.

''There seems like there is something else I should be telling you, but damned if I can think of it.''

''Anything important?'' asked Tynan.

''I doubt it.'' He held out a hand. ''Good luck on this.'' He turned to King. ''Good luck to you too, Doctor.''

''Thank you,'' she said. She then got behind the wheel of one of the jeeps. She started it. The engine caught, ran roughly, belched once, coughing black smoke, and then smoothed out.

''What about fuel?'' asked Tynan.

''There are places to buy it, but there are five-gallon jerry cans in each vehicle. Don't get wild and you should have no problems.''

Tynan hesitated for a moment and then said quietly, ''I think someone broke into my room last night. Searched it carefully and then left.''

''What about King? Anyone bother her?''

''I don't know. I didn't ask because I didn't want to suggest anything to her.''

Cook stood quietly, staring into the distance. Finally he said, ''I'm not sure that this is significant. Almost everyone we send downtown has some kind of trouble like that.

We think it's agents of the local government keeping track of our people—nothing more.''

"Shouldn't you warn us before sending us out?"

Now Cook looked uncomfortable. "We do that and we have people looking under the bed. It's one of those situations where there is no simple solution. Anyway, it's not uncommon, so I wouldn't worry about it.''

"All right," said Tynan. "Seems to be a ridiculous way to handle it."

Cook ignored that and said again, "Good luck."

Tynan got into his jeep. "Thanks again.'' He started his engine and then nodded at King.

She backed out, turned, and started down the curving driveway that led to the street. She stopped at the iron gate. A man came out and opened it but she didn't move until Tynan was right behind her.

The traffic on the wide street was sparse, but King waited for a huge break before pulling out. She slowed once she was in the flow of traffic, waiting until she saw that Tynan was right behind her, and then accelerated.

She weaved her way through the city, along streets that were at first wide, suggesting a modern city, and then narrow, giving a clue to the age. Curving, narrow streets that were built to thwart an invader.

Finally they burst out of the city and into the country. Unlike Vietnam, where the jungle came up to the outskirts of the city, these were open fields. Farmers' huts were scattered around. In the distance was the deep green of the jungle and beyond that was the bright blue of the sky. Huge, white clouds hung low but didn't threaten to storm.

Tynan found himself relaxing. There would be no Vietcong around for an ambush. There would be no mines planted in the middle of the road. Oh, there were stories of roaming Honduran bandits, but it was nothing like the danger presented by the Vietcong or the North Vietnamese in the war zone. It was almost as safe as roaring down the interstate highways in the United States.

He wished there were a commercial broadcast radio in the jeep. The hum of the tires on the concrete was having a hypnotic effect, making him sleepy. He shifted around and glanced over his shoulder. Then, using the rearview mirror, he kept an eye on the highway behind him. Nothing showed in the mirror. No one was following.

He pulled closer to King's vehicle and then dropped back again. He looked at the countryside near the highway. If it hadn't been for the types of trees, the terrain, and the heat and the humidity, Tynan would have believed that he was driving through the Midwest. But these weren't gently rolling plains with large white houses. These were deep green fields spotted with small shacks.

There were tall hills, mountains almost, around them. They descended slowly out of the hills until they reached a flatter, gentler area.

Tynan finally glanced at his watch and noticed that only about two hours had passed. Now in front of him, he could catch occasional glimpses of the Pacific Ocean. It wasn't much more than a thin blue thread on the horizon, quickly lost among the trees and hills, but it was there. The smell of salt and fish began to dominate, blowing inland on a gentle breeze. It seemed cooler, even though they were now at a lower altitude where the humidity should be oppressive. Perhaps a breeze off the ocean had blown the humidity and the heat inland, where it could no longer affect them.

King slowed then, pulling to the side of the road. The shoulder was soft and narrow. The tires on the passenger side sank into the mud, but she didn't seem to notice. She hopped out on her side, showing a lot of her thigh as she climbed out of the jeep. Tynan pulled in behind her but didn't get out.

King leaned an arm against the warm metal of the edge of the windshield and looked in the window at Tynan. "We're going to get to your rendezvous about noon if we're not careful."

Tynan looked at his watch. "What's your point?"

"I just thought you'd want to get there after dark so that no one would see you."

"Well," said Tynan, "I would like to look at it in the daylight so that I can get the lay of the land. We can stop and stroll around and then pile into the jeeps and take off. Later, when I go back, I'll know where I want to park the jeeps and where the best place to wait is."

King shrugged. "Just trying to help."

"Good thinking on your part," said Tynan. "Let's just continue on."

King shrugged and returned to her jeep, and they started off again. They passed through the village of San Lorenzo. At first it wasn't much more than a collection of wooden shacks and stone buildings with thatched roofs. There were poles through the center of town that had wires strung between them in an effort to bring electricity and phone service to the town. The center of the town opened into a wide street where the pavement seemed to thin and crack. There were two- and three-story buildings. A few cars were parked on the street and a few people walked around. There was a long covered porch at the side of what might have been a hotel. People sat there, watching the other people and the traffic.

Across a plaza dotted with huge shade trees was an old church. It was made of adobe, with heavy buttresses and a pointed steeple. There were a couple of huge trees near it, throwing shade on it, and the front doors looked solid enough to withstand a siege.

King pulled to the side of the road and stopped next to a small bus that had once been red but now was a riot of color. There were suitcases, boxes, and woven cages holding birds and pigs strapped to the top. The windows were mostly open and those that weren't were cracked and dirty. There was no one near the bus.

This time when Tynan pulled in behind her, he got out.

As he approached her jeep, she smiled and said, "I bet we could get something to eat at the hotel."

Tynan put a hand to his eyes to shade them and looked at the outdoor restaurant. It looked out of place in the small, dirty village.

"You really want to eat there?"

"Look, Tynan, this is an anthropological expedition. Seeing the natives does not mean standing in the local equivalent of the Holiday Inn and watching them through plate glass. You get out among the people and experience them. Eat what they eat, where they eat it."

"And catch the diseases they catch."

"Jeez, what a pansy. You're not going to catch anything from eating their food."

Tynan opened the door for her and said, "Then lead on."

King swung down out of her jeep and waited while Tynan closed the door. Together they walked to the hotel. The door opened on a small, shabby area where a single couch, one corner propped up on an adobe brick, sat near a window. There was a dying palm in a pot near it. A single man worked behind the desk. Or rather, stood there staring dreamily into space.

They crossed the floor and walked out onto the open-air restaurant. Tynan took a table where he could watch the jeeps, in case some of the locals decided that they needed the supplies stored in the back, but no one approached either vehicle.

For a moment, they sat quietly. Tynan felt the sweat dripping down his sides and beading on his forehead. He noticed the perspiration at King's hairline and the dampening of her shirt under the arms and around the collar. Flies buzzed noisily, and from somewhere came the sounds of a Spanish guitar.

King broke the silence. "So you have a plan?"

"Other than driving by the rendezvous in daylight, not much of one."

"And when the others arrive?"

"Get out of here. Move into the hills again and then stop to wait for daylight."

She poured water from the pitcher sitting on the table and then drank deeply.

"You supposed to drink the water?"

"What the hell difference can it make? You used ice in your drink last night. Where do you think it came from?"

Tynan raised his eyebrows. "Good point."

They lapsed into silence again. They ordered lunch and then ate it quietly and quickly, neither attempting much in the way of conversation. It wasn't an uncomfortable silence, because neither thought of the other as a friend. It was as if two people who barely knew one another shared a table in a crowded diner.

But even with that, Tynan was aware of King. There was no denying that she was a good-looking woman. Her beauty was enhanced by her intelligence. It was an attractive package but Tynan didn't know how to handle the situation. His job, in fact his reason for being there with her, worked against him. She didn't like the thought of the military. And yet, even with the problems that presented, she seemed to be interested in him as a person. There were little signs. Things that she did, some of them unconscious, that said she liked him.

Tynan glanced at her as she bent over her plate. Sweat stood on her face, beading on her upper lip and along her hairline. Perspiration dipped down her neck, disappearing in the V of her shirt.

She looked up and smiled at him. She dropped her eyes quickly, as if embarrassed by the eye contact. Tynan went back to eating, but each time he glanced up, he found her staring at him.

But neither of them spoke, maybe afraid to be the first to express something other than the work relationship that they had established. Tynan wondered if her change in attitude had been the result of orders from the university.

Maybe she had just thought about the situation and decided to change her attitude without the orders.

Or maybe she had an ulterior motive. Maybe she had decided that if she was nicer, it would be easier to get what she wanted, though Tynan wasn't sure what she could want—other than finding the missing people, of course.

He decided that this was not the time to worry about it. He couldn't afford to let his concentration be broken by these thoughts. He had to concentrate on the mission and let King take care of herself.

When he'd finished eating, Tynan said, "Why don't you wait here while I scout the site?"

"Afraid I'll see something I shouldn't?"

"No," said Tynan, shaking his head. "Can't see any reason for the two of us to make the trip. You can sit here, drinking the local beer and seeing the local sights. I shouldn't be gone more than an hour or two."

"You're not afraid that I'll disappear?"

Tynan stood and stared. "Now why in the hell would you disappear?"

She picked up the napkin, moistened it in the water, and dapped it on her neck, lifting her head. She then pulled her shirt away from her body and blew down the front.

"Just a thought," she said.

"I'll meet you here in two hours," said Tynan.

"Two hours."

Tynan made his way from the restaurant, feeling uneasy. He hadn't liked her comment about disappearing, but couldn't figure out a reason why she would want to take off. She would end up alone in the jungle. If the previous expedition of fifteen or twenty couldn't withstand whatever hit them, she wouldn't have a chance alone.

At his jeep he stopped and looked back. She was sitting in the restaurant, staring into space with the same expression that the clerk in the hotel had worn. She was still alone and wasn't even watching him.

Tynan got into his jeep and started the engine. He backed up, turned, and stopped. He glanced at the hotel, but King hadn't moved. He pulled up onto the highway and drove through the town. He stopped on the outskirts and studied the terrain for a moment. Behind him was the town, and in front of him was empty ground. Lush green ground that to the right drifted down to the blue of the Pacific and to the left climbed into the deep blue of the sky. A peaceful, almost gentle landscape that was nearly unchanged since the Mayans and Aztecs had walked it.

He took his foot off the brake and started forward again. The landscape changed slightly. First it was solid ground and then it became marshy and finally swampy. The trees changed, as did the bushes. Spanish moss, looking like decaying skin, hung in great green-gray sheets. The branches became interwoven, forming a loose canopy that blocked out the sky. It was dimmer as the road moved closer to the coast and into the swamp. It became hotter, more oppressive; the humidity was locked in under the trees. It couldn't escape and there was no breeze to blow it free.

Tynan slowed and looked at his map. Now he could hear the surf crashing against the shore. The salt hung in the moist air. There was a rattling in the air above him as monkeys and lizards and birds scrambled from one tree to another.

He had to be close to the top of the gulf. The other SEALS, coming ashore in their rubberized motorboat, would touch ground somewhere nearby. He drove forward slowly, his eyes on the dark, dirty water at the side of the road. The edge of the swamp was a tangle of mangrove roots looking like the gnarled fingers of an ancient giant. Bushes dipped their branches into the water, hiding the dry land from everyone. There was no good place to land.

He kept moving until the nature of the swamp changed. It opened up, so that it was brighter, the water cleaner, the air less foul. He had an unbroken view out to the ocean.

There were currents and eddies visible in the water. There were a hundred places for the SEALS to land, paths from the deep clean water, into the swamp, and then right to the road.

Again he pulled over and studied his surroundings. In the last thirty minutes he hadn't seen another vehicle. By midnight, he hoped that the traffic would be even sparser. He could bring the men right up to the road and load the equipment into the jeeps without having to make a trek through the jungle and swamp. He could wait until there was no one on the highway, and have the men land. They could be out of there in under three minutes.

He found the perfect place then. The road dipped close to the water and then bent back inland. The shoulder seemed to flare outward so that there was a place for him to pull well off the highway. The vegetation was dense enough to hide them, but thin enough that he would be able to see the lights of oncoming traffic. The bank wasn't steep, but slanted gently toward the water. There were no major obstacles in the way and there didn't seem to be any obstructions under the surface of the water.

He nodded and flipped his map closed. He turned around and headed back into San Lorenzo. The afternoon could be spent sitting in the restaurant, drinking beer or Coke while they waited for the midnight rendezvous. Better than crouching in the jungle with a nondirectional beacon, waiting for the enemy to drop on you at any moment while waiting for the drone of aircraft engines.

When he got back to San Lorenzo, he found King's jeep sitting right where they had parked it earlier. He pulled in next to it, feeling a dread drifting over him. But then he got out of the jeep and King was right where she was supposed to be, still alone.

He headed over to the restaurant and slipped into his chair. She glanced at him and smiled. "You get everything you need?"

"I found the perfect place."

"So what do we do now?"

Tynan shrugged. "We wait. That's about all we can do for now."

"Okay. We wait."

6

Tynan arrived at the rendezvous forty minutes early. He pulled his jeep to the side of the road, well off the pavement, and sat there staring into the inky blackness. Without the headlights, there wasn't much difference—shades of dark gray and black, and then a sky filled with stars. Moonlight reflected off the water, in the distance. Tynan had the feeling that he was in a huge cave, the stars no more than a phosphorous display close to his head.

There was little sound: water lapping at the shore; insects buzzing quietly; the deep-throated calls of frogs. He got out of the jeep and stood there scanning the horizon. There was nothing to be seen.

He walked to King's jeep. Over the quiet sound of the idling engine, he said, "I want you to drive about half a mile down the road and then pull over. If anyone comes, blow your horn as soon as they've passed by you."

"There a reason for this?"

"Just one more check. I don't want someone driving by as my men are climbing out of the swamp."

"When do I come back?"

"I'll honk twice. Short blasts. When you hear that, you come on back."

"It seems unnecessarily complicated."

"Maybe," said Tynan, "but it's the way we're going to do it."

King nodded and dropped her jeep into gear. She glanced over her shoulder and then drove back onto the highway. The taillights flashed once and then vanished.

Tynan stood there in the silence of the night and waited. He listened for the sound of the outboard engine on the rubber raft, but it didn't come. Finally, it was midnight, the time for the rendezvous. He took the light from the rear of the jeep and turned toward the open ocean. He flashed the signal Cook had given him: two long, one short, two long.

There was no immediate response. He waited and then ran through it a second time. From out over the water came the shuddering cough of a small engine. It caught, smoothed out, and then nearly faded away.

Tynan stepped back and tossed his light into the jeep. He crouched near it, one hand to his eyes as if to shade them from the stars. He stared into the darkness, searching for the boat. He could hear the quiet buzz of the engine as it came closer. Then, finally, he saw a black shape against the lighter background of the water.

As the boat neared, the engine died, leaving only the natural sounds: water against the shore, insects, frogs, birds, monkeys. There was a quiet noise as the men paddled closer in.

Tynan stepped down, his foot in the water. He reached out, waiting, and then felt his hand grabbed by someone. He leaned back, pulling, and heard the boat scrape up on the soft mud of the shore.

Tynan scrambled up the bank and stopped. He saw one man follow him and then turn, leaning toward the water. Someone grunted and handed something to the man. He tossed it to the side and then reached for something else.

In moments, there was a pile of equipment near the jeep. Tynan waited quietly. As soon as the four men were standing near him, he said, "I'm Tynan."

"Jacobs."

Tynan couldn't tell a thing about the man other than he was huge. He wore black clothing and had his face blackened with camo paint. His voice was quiet and husky and had a slight Southern flavor to it. Not deep South. Maybe Missouri or Northern Kentucky.

"Have your men load the gear into the jeep."

"We have just the one vehicle?"

"There's another down the road." Tynan leaned in and gave the two short blasts.

In seconds, King's jeep was parked facing Tynan's. The men loaded the equipment into the backs of both vehicles. Tynan handed a map to Jacobs and, using a flashlight cupped in his hand so that it was dim, pointed out the route they would follow North into the mountains.

Tynan backed up, turned, and started back down the road. He slowed once, made sure that King and her jeep were close behind, and then sped up. They passed through San Lorenzo again, but turned off the main road. Now they were on a dirt track that led upward into the hills and mountains. The higher they went, the more the road disintegrated.

They left the open fields and meadows and drove into jungle—not thick growth like the central highlands in Vietnam, but a forest of tall trees and huge bushes. It was like driving through a large green tunnel. They slowed as the road became ill defined, but always climbing higher. They came to one wide place. Tynan almost stopped. He turned on the map light and glanced to his right. Jacobs showed him where they were on the chart and Tynan verified that they could drive at least another ten, fifteen miles.

As they continued the journey, each mile coming slower, the jungle grew thicker and the road poorer. Again Tynan stopped and consulted the map. Jacobs worked to keep track of exactly where they were.

Finally the road seemed to end in a wide, shallow pool of stagnant water. Tynan drove along the edge of it until they came to an open field. He drove to the center of it and stopped.

Glancing at his watch, he said, "We'll camp here for the night. Tomorrow we'll head farther inland, driving until we flat can't drive any deeper into the jungle."

Jacobs swung out of his side of the jeep and tossed a couple of satchels to the ground. "Sleeping bag and air mattress," he explained.

"Okay," said Tynan. "I want a guard mounted. One man on watch at all times but not with us. I want him concealed in the trees."

"That shouldn't be a problem," said Jacobs. "Hell, we all slept until starting the run in. Followed all the standard procedures."

"I want us to rest now because I don't know when we'll have a chance again." He hesitated and then added, "I want everyone armed now. Pistols will be fine, but once we start to move, everyone has a rifle too."

He had expected Jacobs to object, but apparently someone had briefed the SEAL on the situation. He merely said, "Aye, aye, Skipper."

Tynan then walked over to King's jeep. The men who had ridden up with her were unloading some of their gear. They were ignoring the woman. As he approached, he heard one of them mumble something about the "ice maiden," but he didn't elaborate.

Tynan stopped close to the door and said, "We'll camp here for the night."

"We can get closer," said King.

"Not tonight," said Tynan. "In the morning, in the daylight, it'll be safer. I don't want to drive over a cliff because we got in a hurry."

King nodded.

"I'll have the men get your sleeping bag and air mattress arranged."

"Don't bother with that," she said. "I'm going to sleep in the jeep."

"You'll be more comfortable in a sleeping bag."

"I'll use the jeep," she said. "I'll be more relaxed in the jeep."

"Have it your way. Oh—I'm posting guards, so don't go wandering around without alerting us."

"You think that's necessary?"

Tynan grinned, knowing that she wouldn't be able to see the gesture in the dark. "We're in the general vicinity where your expedition vanished. What do you think?"

"If you people want to stay up all night playing soldier, you go right ahead."

Tynan shrugged and turned. He moved back and watched as Jacobs and the men set up the camp. Jacobs came over and handed him a pistol.

"Browning nine millimeter," he said. "Fully loaded."

"One in the chamber?"

"Didn't figure to need one in the chamber tonight," said Jacobs.

"You have the guard schedule worked out?"

"Of course. Didn't know if you'd want a turn, so you're scheduled for the last watch, an hour before sun up."

"That's fine," said Tynan. He walked over to the sleeping bag and air mattress that would be his, hoping it wasn't like all the other air mattresses he had seen. Full of slow leaks. It was separated from the jeeps and the others by several feet, a precaution to ensure that an attacker couldn't get them all in a single group. That is, if there was an attacker to worry about.

Tynan took his stand at guard, and then, as the sun came up, he awakened the rest of the party, starting with the huge man nearby. As the man sat up, Tynan asked, "You Jacobs?"

"Sure am. You're Tynan, obviously. Glad to finally be able to put a face with the voice."

"Who you got with you?"

"That's Hernandez over there. Next to him is Lancer and the black man is Jefferson."

"You know what we're here for?"

Jacobs worked his way out of his sleeping bag and stretched. He nodded and said, "Had a complete briefing on the ship last night. Little weird them sending us in, but then, who else they got?"

"I think part of that is my fault. I've done a couple of missions for State and every time they hit a strange one, they call for me. And then I called for help."

"Thanks," said Jacobs. It didn't sound like he meant it, though.

"What's the plan for the day?" asked Jacobs.

"First, breakfast. Then we'll drive as deep into the jungle as we can, walking in from there. With luck we'll be able to find the campsite of the first expedition about midafternoon. From there, we play it by ear."

"Aye, sir."

Tynan stood and moved toward his jeep. The man named Hernandez stood up and looked like he fit in to this part of the world. Short, no more than five foot six or seven, he had dark skin and black hair. He was muscular-looking and Tynan hoped that he could speak Spanish, though no one had mentioned that as being an asset. Now that he thought of it, he wondered why.

Lancer was a tall, thin man, maybe six foot two or three. He had light hair and light skin. The flesh on his face was stretched tight, as though he had been ill recently and not yet fully recovered. His eyes were a dark brown, in sharp contrast to his features.

Jefferson, the final of the new men, was as big as Jacobs. He had short, black hair and dark skin. His features were broad and flat, but his size indicated a heritage that might be traced to the Zulus. He moved with a grace that belied his size.

King opened the door of her jeep and stepped out. She looked at the men and then turned away from them as if embarrassed by being in the jungle with them. Tynan hurried over and said, "We'll want to get going quickly."

"Coffee," she grunted. "Get me coffee first and we can leave."

They had a quick breakfast, the only hot food being the coffee. While they ate, they broke down the camp. Tynan checked the weapon he had been given. Then he got out his web gear, fastened a knife to it that had been brought in with the rest of the weapons. Jacobs gave him an M16.

"We zeroed ours before we got on the airplane. You'll have to hope for the best."

"I'll turn the sniping duties over to you or one of the men. I'll use this like a fire hose."

"Whatever works," said Jacobs.

When they were ready, they moved out again, Tynan in the lead. Jacobs held the map, studying it carefully. Before they had gone too far, Jacobs said, "You know, this map is becoming little more useful than toilet paper."

"Hang on to it anyway," suggested Tynan.

In an hour the jungle had become so thick that the jeeps couldn't go any farther. They stopped in front of a solid wall of green vegetation.

"End of the line," Tynan said.

They all got out and began unloading the equipment, splitting it up equally so that no one had to carry too much. King didn't like that, but understood nonetheless. She shouldered her load and stood quickly, waiting.

Jefferson, a machete in one hand, attacked the vegetation. Tynan used his map and they spread out slowly as they crossed into the denser jungle.

The going at first seemed simple enough; each was well rested. But the longer they walked, the more the humidity got to them. Within thirty minutes, each was covered with sweat. It soaked their clothes and dripped from their faces. Jefferson was rotated out of what would have been point, had they been in combat, replaced by Hernandez.

After an hour, they stopped for a rest. King gulped at

her water, letting it splash down her face and over her chin. She sat with her back against a tree, her eyes closed as she sucked in air.

"You going to be all right?" Tynan asked her.

"I'll be fine," she said.

"Well, don't drink the water so fast and don't waste so much of it. Sources for fresh water are few and far between now."

"I'll be careful," she said without looking at him.

They got going again, moving more slowly this time. Tynan had told them that speed wasn't that important, that nothing was going to get away from them. They cut their way through the jungle, hacking at the vines and the bushes in the way, moving deeper.

At noon, Tynan called a halt and told everyone to eat and rest. He slipped to the ground, using his boonie hat to fan his face for what little relief it created. As he sat there, he was suddenly aware of something new, something of an undertone in the jungle—a quiet, distant rumbling.

And then, the light breeze brought an odor that he couldn't fail to recognize. He slipped off his pack and stood up, turning slowly until the breeze was hitting him in the face.

Jacobs moved toward him, but Tynan held up a hand and nodded. He knew what the other SEAL was going to say.

"We're close."

"How you want to handle this, Skipper?"

"Let's leave everyone else here while you and I press on. We have to be within a hundred yards of the expedition site."

Jacobs stood, his hands on his hips, and studied the jungle around them. He pointed: "Seems that there's a clearing in that direction."

Tynan reached down and picked up his M16. He caught King's look and said, "You wait here."

"If you've found something," she protested, "then I want to be part of it."

Tynan held up a hand to stop her. "You wait here while we check this out. We'll be back just as soon as we confirm that we've reached the site."

She looked like she was going to protest again, but then simply nodded. "All right."

Jacobs moved toward Hernandez, talked with him quietly, and then said, "I'm all set."

Tynan led the way deeper into the bush, using his machete to chop at the vines and bushes. He was making noise as he slashed through the vegetation, something that bothered him, but he kept telling himself that he wasn't in Vietnam and noise discipline wasn't critical here.

He stopped, touching his forehead to the sleeve of his fatigue jacket. The odor was getting stronger. Through the gaps in the vegetation, he could begin to catch glimpses of the clearing. No detail yet, but he knew he was getting close.

He turned to Jacobs and told the bigger man that they were near the site where the first expedition had been attacked.

Jacobs shrugged. "That's good. I can use the rest."

Tynan swung his machete and the branch of a bush fell away. Tynan stepped forward and then dropped to one knee. He kept telling himself that he wasn't in Vietnam, but a feeling of anxiety kept pressing in on him. He fingered the butt of the rifle slung over his back, then got to his feet and moved forward again.

Around him was the penetrating odor of death. It was a stench blown on the breeze. He knew exactly what it signaled and wondered if it was the reason that he felt uneasy.

And then he became aware of the drums: a quiet rumbling that he could barely hear; a beat, a rhythm that seemed to be sinister. Maybe it was meant as a warning.

He slipped the machete into the sheath and unslung his

M16, making sure that a round was chambered. Without a word to Jacobs, Tynan had decided it was now a combat patrol. Noise discipline was suddenly important. He wouldn't leap into the clearing like an untrained civilian. He'd approach it in a military manner.

Glancing over his shoulder, he saw that Jacobs had picked up on the signals. Jacobs had his weapon ready and was crouched near the trunk of a mahogany tree, his back to it.

Tynan moved forward slowly, putting his foot down carefully, rolling it from heel to toe. He was aware of the animals around him. Lizards scrambling through the canopy over him. Birds, some sitting and squawking, some flying and landing. Monkeys called to one another, insects buzzed.

He kept going, watching everything around him, until he reached the edge of the clearing, where he crouched. Spread out in front of him were the remains of the camp. The tents still stood, but the material had been slashed so that it flapped in the breeze. Equipment had been smashed and pieces of it littered the ground. There were overturned pots, wood fragments that had been desks or tools or chairs. There were books torn apart and thrown everywhere. The radio was smashed into a lump of brightly colored plastic and wire.

And there were bodies. Bloated bodies, swollen by the build up of internal gasses. The buttons of shirts had popped. The material of shorts had split.

And there was the sound of flies—hundreds of thousands of them.

Tynan rubbed his chin with the edge of his hand and took a deep breath. He immediately regretted it as the odor of death filled his nostrils.

"That's them," said Jacobs, his voice quiet.

"I think that completes our mission," said Tynan.

"We going to go in and take a closer look?"

Tynan wanted to shake his head, but knew that they'd

have to. And then they'd probably have to remain until the American Embassy could get someone out to deal with the problem. It meant they would have to stay on the site with death all around them. It wasn't a task he wanted to perform.

"Let's slip back," said Tynan, "and get the others. Let King identify the bodies and see if we can determine what happened here."

"They had to be attacked," said Jacobs.

"That goes without saying," snapped Tynan, and then regretted saying it.

"Just making conversation."

Tynan slipped to the rear, away from the clearing. He took point, keeping his rifle ready. He was sweating heavily and not all of it was the heat and humidity of the jungle. Some of it was tension. The drumming was louder now. He didn't have to strain to hear it anymore. It surrounded him like a thick audible fog.

They followed the path they had created back to where the others waited. That too was something Tynan wouldn't have done in Vietnam. Following the same path invited ambush, but then, he wasn't in Vietnam, and as far as he knew, there was no one around to ambush him. He had to kept reminding himself of that fact.

They came to the others. Hernandez and King were sitting on a rotting log, eating from C-ration cans, using the white plastic spoons that came with the rations. Hernandez's weapon was close at hand and if it hadn't been for King sitting beside him, he would have looked like a soldier on patrol in Vietnam. The woman gave the picture an unreal quality.

As soon as Tynan and Jacobs appeared, King was on her feet. "You found them?"

Tynan nodded. "It's as bad as we've assumed. They're dead. Bodies are there."

"All of them?" asked King.

"We didn't enter the camp yet." Tynan moved to the

log and sat down. "Tents are still standing, but they've been torn up. The equipment was thrown all over the place and the camp was wrecked."

King nodded solemnly. "Radio reports seemed to suggest that."

"Yeah," said Tynan. "Still, until you see it, there's always the possibility that you've misinterpreted what you heard. Now . . ." He let his voice trail off.

"What do we do now?" asked King.

"Get everyone together and move to the camp. Set up there and examine it carefully. See if we can figure out what happened and why it happened." Tynan looked at Hernandez. "Where are the others?"

"In the jungle keeping watch. I didn't want anyone to sneak up on us."

"Good," said Tynan. He turned his attention back to King. "What is with those drums, anyway?"

"I don't know," she said. But she did. The Mayans had used drums as part of their ritual before offering sacrifices to their gods. Copán, a huge Mayan city fifteen hundred years ago, wasn't more than fifty miles away. It was the site of hundreds, maybe thousands of bloody rituals in which human lives were sacrificed to the gods.

7

Tynan led the team to the edge of the clearing and then stopped. The other SEALS fanned out, taking up positions to guard one another just as if this were a combat patrol in Vietnam and not a search party in Central America. Tynan crouched there, with King by his side, studying the mess left in the clearing.

King gasped once as she saw one of the bodies, but then was silent. Her face was a mask, unreadable.

Tynan turned and pointed to Jacobs. Together, along with Jefferson, they moved into the clearing. Tynan led the way, moving slowly toward the closest body. As he neared it, he could only tell that it was female. The features on the face were distorted and the hair was matted with dried blood. She had a wound on her forehead that was alive with buzzing flies and a massive injury to her chest. The ground around her was a rusty black as the flies crawled in her blood. Tynan didn't bother to check to see if she were still alive. It was obvious that she wasn't.

Jefferson and Jacobs checked the other bodies, moving from one to another, knowing by the stench and the flies and the time that had passed that no one in the clearing lived.

While they did that, Tynan searched through the tents, but there was nothing of value left in them. Cots, desks, packs, and clothes had been shredded and destroyed. Papers were thrown everywhere. Notebooks were torn apart. Equipment was broken. Someone had swept through the camp, destroying everything in it.

He worked his way through, checking each of the tents, but not touching anything. He came to another body—a young man who had been wearing only shorts. His feet were swollen and purpled. There was a single large wound to his back exposing his spine and rib cage. The flies hovered near him, buzzing loudly as they dived at the wounds.

He stopped at the far end of the clearing, looking back at the destruction. Not random destruction that would suggest animals, but a deliberate destruction that suggested humans. Tynan turned and glanced at the jungle, but he saw nothing that told him where the killers had come from or where they had waited in ambush.

As he walked back, he was aware of the drums pounding away. He stopped once and cocked his head but couldn't pick up a direction. They seemed to come from everywhere, as if the clearing was ringed with speakers.

When he reached the center of the camp, he stopped. Jacobs moved toward him and said, "Someone took a machete to the radio. I doubt we could find enough pieces to make a crystal set work right."

"Destruction seems to be systematic."

"Jefferson counted twelve bodies lying around." He stared at the tents and then said, "Anyone in there?"

"No."

"Then we're short what—four, five people?"

"Yeah, something like that. Listen, I think you'd better get Lancer and Hernandez out as security. Someone attacked these people and I don't want the same someone slipping up on us."

"What about King?"

Tynan shrugged. "We'll have to get her in to identify

the dead and see if she can help us figure out the next move.''

''Hernandez is a crackerjack tracker. Grew up in west-Texas hanging around all those Comanche Indians. There's nothing he can't track if he puts his mind to it.''

Tynan pointed. ''All this happened—what, four days, five days ago. There won't be much in the way of signs left for him to follow.''

Jacobs said, ''He doesn't need much.''

''Then let him see what he can do.''

Jacobs moved off then, signaling the rest of the men out of the jungle. King came with them, a handkerchief to her nose to try to filter the odor of death. Her eyes were wide, as if she were afraid of what she was seeing.

''Come on, Doctor,'' said Tynan. ''You've seen dead bodies before.''

''Not like these.''

Tynan stepped in front of her and grabbed her shoulders. ''Get a grip. There's nothing we can do for them here. We've got to search the area and then get assistance in here. You need to help.''

She stood staring, almost like a stone statue. Then she blinked and seemed to come out of it. ''Moore, the expedition leader, should have been keeping records. It might tell us something.''

''Which one is Moore?''

King stood and then slowly turned, her eyes resting briefly on each of the bodies. Finally she shrugged. ''He's not here. He's not here.''

''Yeah,'' said Tynan. ''We figure there are four or five who aren't here.''

''Then they're alive!''

''I don't want to deflate your balloon,'' said Tynan, ''but just because their bodies aren't here, doesn't mean they're alive.''

''Sure it does,'' said King. ''They have to be alive.''

''No,'' insisted Tynan. He wasn't sure whether he should

drive home the truth, or if he should let her cling to the little hope that some of her friends might be alive. Reality or fantasy. He didn't know which was better for her.

She moved away from him, stopping at the body of the woman. She pointed at the chest wound and asked, "Don't you recognize this?"

"I see a body that's been mutilated."

"No," she said, her voice taking on added authority. "It's classic Mayan."

"What?"

"The wound," she said, sounding like she was lecturing a class in the States. "The Mayans were famous for it. Well, so were the Aztec and the Toltec, but the Mayans, just before the collapse of their civilization, seemed to go on an orgy of sacrificial murder. They'd torture the victims in horrible fashion and then cut out their hearts following a strict, bloody custom. Just like here."

"Come on," said Tynan. "There are no Mayans left."

"Well," said King, "that's technically not true. There are people in the region who can trace their heritage to the Mayans and who can speak a form of the language. Some of that heritage has been passed from generation to generation."

"So what you're telling me is that the Mayans, a civilization that everyone thinks was destroyed when the Spanish landed, still exists."

"No," she said, excited. "You don't get it, do you? I'm saying there's a pocket of people around here who have kept some of the traditions alive. Look around you. It's obvious."

"The only thing obvious here is that someone has killed a number of your fellow scientists and destroyed their camp and equipment."

King seemed to have passed beyond the emotions that confirmation of the worst had brought. It was as if she had always expected the worst, and having found it, she wasn't overwhelmed by it. It was a strange reaction for a lady who had been raised in the United States, where most violence was televised and most death sanitized. Tynan had expected her to fall apart when she viewed the broken, mutilated bodies of her fellow scientists. That hadn't been the case.

Now, with the answer spread out in front of her, she was no longer worried about them, seemed more concerned with the things that she could learn, more concerned with her theory. She moved across the camp, passed the remains of the camp fire with the melted lump of metal that had been the coffeepot, and walked toward the body of the man near the radio.

She crouched near the body, then looked up, her eyes shining—not with tears, but excitement. "He was decapitated. The Mayans often decapitated their victims."

"In their rituals," Tynan protested, not sure that he was right about that or not.

"Maybe," said King. "But in battle, they were fierce fighters."

"This was no battle."

King stood and moved again. She stopped and looked at the destruction. "But to them it was a battle. An invasion. They would want to destroy everything that the invaders brought with them except those things that they could use themselves. I'll wager that you found no knives, axes, or shovels among the debris."

"We haven't looked."

"Don't bother. You won't find anything like that. The Mayan culture didn't have any metallurgy. They worked in stone. Obsidian and flint and jade. The metal items our people brought would become priceless to them."

Tynan finally held up a hand. "Look, Stevie, you've grabbed at a straw here and built a whole foundation on it. Not a solid way to work." He wasn't sure that he liked the way she was so coldly evaluating the evidence. These had been her friends, not people she had never known.

"You hear the drums?" she asked.

"Of course."

"Mayans. They signal the beginnings of the rituals. They need victims for them, humans to sacrifice. That will be our missing people."

"No," said Tynan. "I just don't believe that."

"You idiot. The evidence is all around you. Who do you think did this?"

"Bandits," said Tynan. "The hills are filled with them, just as they are throughout central Mexico. Bandits who saw easy pickings and who swooped in on the expedition."

"Bandits," she sneered. "You've been watching too many adventure movies. Bandits wouldn't be able to survive around here because there is no one for them to prey on. Bandits."

Jacobs appeared then. "Hernandez says he can't find any sign around here. It's been too long and there are too many animals in the region."

"Okay," said Tynan. "Let's get the radio set up and make contact with the embassy. Let them know what all we've found here."

"And then?"

"Make arrangements to get us and the bodies moved out of here."

"But we have to search for the missing people," said King. "We've got to find them." She pointed to the trees. "It's our responsibility to find them."

"Let's just make radio contact and see what they have to say. Besides, we don't know where to look for the missing people."

"Not true," said King. "I know exactly where to look. Besides, think of the headlines if we find a Mayan city that's still inhabited. World fame."

Tynan ignored that. Instead, he told Jacobs to get the radio set up and they'd take their orders from the embassy.

"I want to talk to them."

"You can't be serious about pulling out," said King, her voice rising. "There is so much that we must do."

"Our job was to determine the status of the missing expedition and we've done that."

"But there are people still missing. You have an obligation to find them. You can't just get out now."

"We can do just that," responded Tynan. "We can get out just as we were ordered to do."

"Not without telling someone that a few people might still be living. I demand the right to speak on your radio."

Tynan bowed in her direction and said, "And be sure to let Dr. King talk to them."

"Aye, aye, Skipper."

Brian Moore sat on the cold stone of the floor and listened to the water dripping somewhere. He couldn't see it because the cell was locked in darkness. He thought, however, that he could see shapes and shadows as the others moved about. There was straw spread on the floor and there was a hole cut in it in a corner. A cold draft smelling of urine and feces blew up from below.

Moore shifted around again and leaned to the rear, bracing his back against the wall. Solid rock with only the thinnest of joints between the stones. He had been able to find the joints only by running his fingertips over the stone. It was a well-constructed cell and there was no way out, except through the stone door that was impossible to move.

The other two in there with him—Sara Robinson and Jason Hughes—hadn't spoken for several hours. Upon arrival, they had been amazed and hadn't been able to stop talking about the discovery. The fact that the city was still inhabited and hadn't been seen by outsiders for centuries had overshadowed the horrible deaths of their co-workers.

But all that had worn off as they had been dragged down the rock-lined corridors, away from the sun and light, and locked in the cell. Moore and Hughes had worked their way around the whole cell, feeling every square inch of it, looking for an avenue of escape, but had found none.

Sara had slumped to the floor, pulled her knees up, and wrapped her arms around her legs. She tried not to cry, but the events of the morning were too fresh in her mind. She saw Linda cut down by a man with a bow and arrow. She had seen the man leap to the wounded Linda, roll her to her back, and then slash at her chest with a dull-colored knife. He had ripped her still-beating heart from her body and held it aloft as if it were some kind of trophy.

Now the horror of the scene filled her head and she couldn't shake it. The fear that had kept it suppressed, as they were led through the jungle like lambs to the slaughter, was gone. Everything was gone. All she could do was sit on the cold floor, in the dark, and cry.

Moore had finally sat down beside her, putting an arm around her for comfort, but had said nothing. She turned her face toward him and sobbed until she knew that she could cry no more.

"What's going to happen to us?" she demanded.

And although Moore had a very good idea, he said, "I don't know."

He wished that he had studied the Mayan calendar more thoroughly. In it were the clues to their fate. They would become sacrifices to the various Mayan gods, but the ceremonies were so ritualized that he didn't know how long they would be held. It might be mere hours, in which case, there would be no hope for rescue, or it might be weeks, which meant that someone might reach them.

Hughes kept prowling the cell, feeling the walls and the floor and the door. He would sit down for a few minutes and then would be up again, walking around the cell, touching it. He tripped once and fell with a loud thump. He cried out in surprise and pain, but then was silent.

Finally, Robinson had pushed herself away from Moore and stood up. "I'll be fine now," she announced, though her voice was shaky.

Moore had no idea how long they had been in the cell. The luminous dial on his watch slowly faded until he could no longer see it. Neither Hughes nor Robinson had managed to get to their watches before the world had disintegrated.

Their captors had slid the massive stone blocking the entrance out of the way once, given them earthenware bowls filled with a warm soup made from corn. They had said nothing and had slipped the stone back into place after setting the bowls on the floor.

When they had finished eating, Moore decided that it was his job to cheer up his fellows. He sat in the corner and said, ''We have a unique opportunity here.'' He waited and when neither commented, he added, ''We have found the remnants of a civilization that was supposed to have disappeared five hundred years ago. Think of the opportunity we have to enrich our knowledge of the era.''

He knew he sounded ridiculously pompous, but he wanted to take their minds off the situation, if only for a few moments. Let them begin to think like the scientists they claimed to be. Let them analyze rationally all that they were seeing and hearing.

''What's going to happen to us?'' Robinson finally asked.

''I think that the priest class will want to talk to us and if we can make ourselves understood, I think we'll be okay. I think we'll be able to convince them to let us go.''

''You really believe that?'' asked Robinson.

''Naturally,'' Moore said, though he knew it wouldn't happen. They'd be taken to the top of one of the pyramids and killed, just as thousands of others had been, unless someone showed up to rescue them, which was highly unlikely. Even if someone came, it would probably be another team of scientists from the university, when it was obvious that soldiers were needed.

Lancer set up the radio in the middle of the clearing, where it would be the safest. No one could approach them easily without being seen. No one would get within fifty yards if Lancer and the others decided he shouldn't.

To set up the radio, he had extended the antenna, not worrying about the tricks to prevent triangulation that he would have used in Vietnam. He sat down next to it, switched it on, using a battery pack to power it, and made his initial call.

King sat next to him, her legs folded under her Indian fashion, one elbow on the side of her knee and her chin cupped in her hand as she waited her turn.

As soon as Lancer had made contact, he held the handset up. "You want to talk to them, Skipper?"

Tynan walked over and took the handset. "We're on site and have twelve dead and five missing."

"Roger that," said the voice that Tynan recognized as Cook's.

"Will stay here until arrangements to remove the dead can be made."

There was a long pause and Tynan wondered if they had lost radio contact. He looked at Lancer, who shrugged and said quietly, "It's not us."

Finally, as Tynan was about to repeat his message, he heard, "Be advised that you are to abandon site and search for possible survivors."

"Negative," said Tynan. "I said nothing about survivors. We have missing bodies."

King glared at him.

Again there was a hesitation and Tynan realized that Cook was talking to someone who was getting instructions from somewhere else. Just what he wanted. Nine hundred different people trying to make decisions without having all the facts. But then, they weren't going to be inconvenienced or killed by those bad decisions.

"Is Dr. King available?"

Tynan gave her the handset. He pointed to the side and said, "You squeeze it there to talk, and release it when you've finished."

"This is Dr. King, over."

"Please advise on situation at your end."

She hesitated, looked at Tynan, and said, "Can you repeat that, over."

Tynan groaned inwardly. *Repeat* on a military radio meant that they wanted another six rounds from the artillery. No one said, "Repeat." They said, "Say again."

"Do you believe that the missing people are dead or alive?"

"Alive!" she nearly shouted. "We've not found the bodies and I believe they were captured."

"Understood," said Cook at the far end. "Please wait one."

King looked at Tynan again. "He means to hold on for a moment."

"Please advise people with you that a search for the missing scientists will be undertaken with all possible haste."

"Yeah," said King. She pointed to the radio. "Now you have your orders."

Tynan took the handset and asked, "What is the disposition of the bodies?"

"Cover them as best you can. Arrangements are being made to get them out of there."

"Roger."

Tynan looked at King, but she didn't have anything more to say. There was nothing he wanted from the embassy. He gave the handset back to Lancer and let him finish up.

As he walked away from the radio, King caught him and said, "What are we going to do now?"

"We've only got about three hours until dark. We'll have to get the bodies pulled together and cover them with the remains of the tents. Tomorrow, just after sunrise, we'll want to begin the search." He shook his head. "That's going to be a real mess. I have no idea where to look."

"I think I might," said King.

Tynan stopped walking and asked, "And just where might that be?"

"The original destination. If Moore had to abandon the camp and couldn't get back to the roads or civilization, I think he would have pushed on toward the lost city. It would be the one place that we could look for him."

"That makes no sense," said Tynan. "If he could make the lost city, why couldn't he get back to the roads? After seeing his friends cut down, why would he press on?"

"I don't know," said King, "but I think we should search in that direction."

"Well, not tonight," said Tynan. "Tonight we stay here. I want you to search through the papers and notebooks and see if you can piece together what happened. Failing that, I want you to decide what needs to be saved so that we can take it with us. The rest will be gathered to go out with the bodies."

Jacobs moved in and asked, "What do you want us to do?"

"Let's get the bodies moved together and covered with what's left of the tents. Then we'll mount a guard and wait out the night. Tomorrow we'll get going again."

"Aye, sir," said Jacobs.

"We've got a lot of work to do before nightfall," said Tynan.

"And we caught one break," said Jacobs. "That breeze is making it possible for us to stay up here. If it wasn't for that, we'd have to get out."

"Get a fire burning and throw on some wet wood. That should take that odor out of the air," said Tynan.

"Now if we only had something to drown out those damn drums," said Jacobs.

"They do get on your nerves, don't they?"

8

The drums kept beating throughout the night. Sometimes they quieted enough so that Tynan had to strain to hear them. And each time they faded, that was exactly what he did. He wanted to make sure that they hadn't stopped altogether, afraid that when they did something would happen.

Tynan found himself relaxing; the beat of the drums had a hypnotic effect, but just when he was about to go under, the rhythm would change. It was always subtle, but enough to bring him back. Maybe that was the source of his anxiety.

The night seemed to stretch forever. The fire they had built, filling the clearing with a woodsmoke that almost overpowered the odor of death around them, burned down. The flickering cast fleeting, shifting shadows that Tynan soon learned to ignore.

He listened to the other sounds. The howl of a huge cat, maybe a jaguar. King had told him that the Mayans had a cult of were-jaguars—old spirits that could inhabit the bodies of men, changing them into jaguars. Much of the art associated with later Mayan periods had that motif. It was obvious on the stone carvings and the jade masks.

Tynan kept telling himself he was safer in the jungle in Honduras than he would be in New York City. Here he was armed. In New York they frowned on weapons. And he was definitely safer than he would be in Vietnam.

But somehow, that didn't comfort him. The drums kept hammering away, filling the night with an undefinable terror. They were all affected by it. He could tell. Jacobs sat near the fire, using a whetstone to sharpen a knife that already put a scapel to shame. Lancer went out to relieve Hernandez on guard duty early. And King just walked around the perimeter of the camp, staying in the shadow.

Finally, at four, Tynan could take it no longer. He sat up, checked his weapon, and stood. He walked toward the fire and bent close to it, feeling the heat from the coals. He glanced at King and saw that she too was awake. He moved toward her, sat down, and asked, "You learn anything?"

She sat up and rubbed the heels of her hands in her eyes. She blinked rapidly and then sighed. "Learn anything?" she repeated, her voice low.

"About the first expedition?"

"Nothing that will help us. Standard notes about the route of travel and the environment." She grinned, her teeth white in the dim light of false dawn. "Kind of overwritten. Tells about how thick the jungle is. Talks about the tall mahogany trees and the thick undergrowth."

"Anything else?"

She didn't answer right away, and then said, "The drums. He mentions the drums, but not until the night before they vanished."

"Then they mean something?"

"I don't know. I don't think so. It's not like the Old West where the Sioux dance all night and when the drums stop, they attack the fort."

"You're saying that there is no significance to the drums, then?"

"I'm saying nothing of the sort. I'm saying that I don't know if there is a connection between them and what happened here."

Tynan stood up. "It's about an hour to dawn. We get up now, break camp and eat breakfast, we can be off with the first light."

For a moment it looked as if she were going to say something else. The flickering of the firelight highlighted her features. Tynan was aware of her as a woman for that moment. He found his eyes on her legs and then at her chest.

She smiled shyly, as if she understood exactly what he was thinking, and approved. Finally she said, "Okay. We're off at first light."

"Stevie, I want you to know one thing." He had been going to say something about their relationship, about what he was thinking, and then suddenly decided that the time wasn't right. Instead, he told her, "I think this is a wild goose chase. If I had my way, we'd stay here until the next party arrives and then evacuate with them."

"But you're going through with it?"

"Of course. I have my orders."

He moved away then. He crouched near Jacobs and touched the SEAL on the foot. Jacobs came awake instantly. "Yeah?"

"Let's get ready to pull out of here. Eat breakfast and be ready to go at first light."

Jacobs rubbed a hand through his hair and sat quietly for a moment. "Damn drums haven't stopped, have they?"

"You afraid the Indians are going to attack."

"Hell, Skipper, who knows what's going to happen."

Tynan moved away and saw a shadow moving across the open ground, running in a semi-crouch. Tynan dropped to one knee, his hand on the safety of his M16, waiting until he identified the target. Hernadez stopped near him.

"I've got movement out there."

"Where?"

Hernandez glanced over his shoulder and said, "Back in that direction. Four, maybe five guys, moving real quiet.

They're very good and use the natural sounds in the jungle to mask their movement.''

"They coming this way?"

"More or less. I stayed put until I was sure that they weren't moving away from us, or that they wouldn't pass us on one side or the other."

"Shit," said Tynan.

"My sentiments exactly."

Tynan rubbed his mouth with his fingers. He heard a whisper of noise caused by the stubble on his face. "We've got to assume the worst. That first expedition didn't and we've seen the results of that."

"Yes, sir."

Tynan whirled and hurried toward the center of the camp. He crouched there and whispered, "Let's get moving. People are coming at us."

"Who?" demanded King, her voice high and tight.

"I would assume the same people who visited your expedition," said Tynan.

"How we going to handle this, Skipper?" asked Jacobs.

"Ambush them first." He thought about that and said, "No. We've got to let them make the first hostile move. Then we ambush them."

"You can't," said King.

"Oh, but we can. That's why we were brought in on this. If everyone in Washington and at your university thought that it was completely safe, then they wouldn't have called us. They wanted someone who could handle a hostile enemy force without getting a lot of our people killed."

"So what do we do?" asked Jacobs.

Tynan grinned in the growing dawn. "The oldest trick in the book. Stuff the sleeping bags with leaves and rags and whatever to make it look like we're still here. Build up the fire and then we go hide in the jungle. See what happens."

"That one's so old it has whiskers on it," said Jacobs.

"Of course, but look at it this way: these guys blew in last time, found everything here the way they expected it to be, and killed everyone they could find. They won't expect us to get fancy.''

"I'll get Lancer in—"

"No, leave him out there for the time being." Tynan pointed at Hernandez and Jefferson. "Start stuffing the sleeping bags. I'll grab some wood."

As Tynan turned to move, Hernandez and Jefferson leaped to work. King stood there watching until she could stand it no more. She then joined the two men as they arranged the camp.

Tynan started throwing wood into the camp fire. For a moment nothing much happened. Then smoke poured from it and flames began to crackle.

"Let's move it," said Tynan.

They grabbed their weapons and packs, and Hernandez picked up the radio. They scrambled across the clearing, entering the jungle near Lancer. The SEAL came out of hiding and asked, "What the hell?"

"Someone's coming," whispered Jacobs. "We're just going to see who they are."

Tynan said, "Spread out along the edge of the trees, but not so far apart that we can't support one another."

"What about King?" asked Jacobs.

"I'll keep her near me." Tynan glanced at her and then said, "We're just going to watch and we'll need you to remain quiet. If those people show hostile intent and come at us, we'll take them out."

Jacobs slipped to the right and dropped to the ground, moving farther so that he was under the flowing branches of a fern.

Tynan grabbed King's hand and dragged her along the tree line. He found a shallow depression protected by the roots of a huge tree. He pushed her into it. "Stay there. If there's any shooting, keep your head down."

With that, Tynan moved to the other side of the tree. He

knelt there, listening to the sounds around him: the animals moving quietly, the light breeze rattling the leaves, and the drums that had yet to stop.

The sky changed from black to gray and then reds and oranges. The ground brightened slowly. Objects in the clearing began to take shape. In the light of the fire, he could see the sleeping bags, which somehow looked unnatural. Maybe it was the way that they had stuffed them. It didn't seem possible that anyone would be fooled.

He slowly lowered himself until he was resting on his stomach, watching for the enemy. Not enemy he reminded himself, but the people who were coming.

It was hard to get his mind off the idea that the men coming were the enemy. He had seen the results of the last contact between these people and intruders from the United States. He didn't believe this would be any different.

Movement across the clearing caught his attention—a phantom shape that disappeared quickly. He focused his attention on that section of the jungle and moments later saw one man step into the clearing. He stopped there, crouched, and waited, maybe wondering if Tynan and his party had guards out.

Of course, there was no response. The man stood and moved forward slowly, stepping carefully. His head seemed to swivel from side to side as if searching the ground for something. In the growing light, Tynan could see that he did not wear the standard peasant clothes. Instead, the man seemed to be wearing a knee-length toga with shoulder and chest pads. He carried a spear, the point held down.

As he approached the campsite, others joined him, fanning out behind him. All were similarly attired, though not all of them were armed with spears. A couple carried machetes and one held a bolo, the weights swinging gently where they hung down.

King gasped once, quietly, and then became to creep forward as if to see better. She reached out and pushed the branches of a bush aside.

Tynan wanted to knock her down, stop her from mov- ing, but didn't want to move. King stopped then, watching as the men advanced across the clearing.

In Vietnam, Tynan would have burned them. Cut them down once they were easy targets, but here, he couldn't do that. He had to let them make their move, and even when they did, he wasn't sure how to react.

There were now a dozen men in the clearing, sweeping up the gentle slope to the camp. They moved steadily, their gazes fixed on the supposed slumbering shapes of the people in the sleeping bags. In the background the pound- ing of the drums seemed to get louder, as if the drummers knew that something was about to happen.

The men stopped, crouched, and searched the ground around them. The sun continued to rise, the horizon now glowing. A light white fog filtered out of the jungle, obscuring some of the clearing, giving the scene a surreal look.

The hammering of the drums seemed to peak and as it did, the men struck. There was no warning. They leaped the last few feet and attacked the sleeping bags. They hacked at them with their machetes and stabbed at them with their spears. A few of the men ran beyond, as if establishing a perimeter.

Tynan wanted to open fire. He wanted to kill them before they had a chance to retreat into the jungle. But he didn't shoot. He stayed where he was, watching something that he would have believed belonged in the ancient past. Mayan warriors attacking the camp of interlopers.

The plan sprang into his mind full blown. They would hang back, let the enemy retreat into the jungle and then follow them to their camp. It had to be where the missing people, if they were alive, were being held. It simplified his orders.

But then King was on her feet and moving again. She burst from the cover and took a few steps into the clearing. The sunlight, slanting through the trees illuminated her as if it were a spotlight she had stepped into. She stood still, one hand raised in greeting and called out in a strange language. Tynan had never heard anything like it.

The men had finished hacking at the sleeping bags and were ripping them apart as if angered by the trick. They stopped when King appeared. The men on the perimeter crouched, their spears up as if expecting an attack. No one moved for a moment.

Tynan was up and moving then, working his way through the jungle until he was at the edge of the trees, almost directly behind King. He halted there, waiting for the Mayans to take action.

The whirring sound that he had heard on the tape of the first attack came then. A strange noise that built quickly. Tynan suddenly realized what it was. He glanced to the right and saw one of the Mayan there, the bolo slashing through the air over his head as he prepared to throw it.

Tynan leaped from his cover and tackled King. She fell heavily, first to her knees and then to her side as she twisted around. She grunted in surprise and the breath whistled through her nostrils. She gasped for air as the bolo cut the air over them and slammed into one of the trees behind them, winding itself around the trunk.

When that failed to kill either King or Tynan, the remainder of the men attacked, whooping and yelling. They held their spears high overhead and ran across the clearing.

Tynan came up on one knee and aimed. King squirmed around and tried to shout at him. She started to reached out, but the report from his weapon startled her.

Tynan fired once, saw the man closest to him drop and roll. The other Mayan didn't hesitate. He rushed onward, screaming. Firing broke out in the jungle behind Tynan. Single shots, spaced randomly as the men there found their targets. The Mayans fell, blood spurting. There were cries of surprise and pain, but they came on. None of them wanted to show fear.

Tynan tried to drag King into the safety of the trees. She

jerked her hand away from him and hugged the ground. She refused to move. Tynan crouched over her, using his rifle. He fired again, saw that man fall and swung around. One of the Mayans had come from no where and was nearing on him. Tynan dived to his left and rolled to his back. He pulled the trigger twice, the bullets slamming into the thick leather padding of the warrior's chest. The Mayan dropped his spear and grabbed at his wounds as he fell forward.

The firing from the trees began to taper off. Tynan was up again, searching the field. The bodies of the Mayans were scattered in a ragged line from the sleeping bags to near where King and Tynan were.

Tynan got to his feet and stepped to the closest man. He probed with the toe of his boot, but could tell the man was dead. The entrance holes might be small, but the exit wounds were massive. The blood was pooled under the man already.

Jacobs and Hernandez left the trees and began to work their way across the field, picking up the weapons and checking the bodies.

"Why?" demanded King.

Tynan looked down on her. Her face was pale and her eyes were wide. "Why?" he repeated. "Because you had to talk to them. You had to come out of hiding."

"That's no excuse. We could have talked to them."

"Before or after they killed us?"

She got to her feet and brushed at her clothes. Her hair hung down in her face. "You didn't have to be so rough," she said.

Jacobs reappeared. "There are two wounded, but Jefferson doesn't think they'll last long. One took a round through the stomach and is in a lot of pain."

"There anything Jefferson can do for them?"

"I don't think so."

"What are you planning to do?" asked King. "Kill them?"

"You know," said Tynan, "if they were animals, people would think us humane for putting them out of their misery. But because they're people, we have to let them suffer, knowing full well that there is nothing we can do to save them. They'll die soon enough."

King said, "Let me look at them. Maybe I can help."

"You have medical training?" asked Jacobs.

"No, not really."

"Well, Jefferson has medical training and there's nothing he can do for them."

She didn't answer. She just walked off, heading for the wounded men.

"What now, Skipper?"

"I would assume that Hernandez now has a trail he can follow."

"I think that's right."

"Then we've got our first real clue. King said she thought the missing people might be held in that city they were heading for. If the trail leads in that direction, then we may have our answer."

"What about the wounded?" Jacobs asked.

"We'll make them as comfortable as we can and then we'll get out of here. I'll want to put some distance between us and this site. Then we'll think about breakfast."

"Aye, aye, sir."

9

It took only a few minutes to get organized. Jacobs and his men dragged the bodies of the dead Mayan warriors into the jungle so that they weren't in plain sight. King collected the weapons, marveling over them because they were advanced far beyond anything that the Mayans were thought to possess. Once or twice she'd tried to mention that, but Tynan had told her to hurry. They didn't have time to mess around studying the craftsmanship of the weapons.

She had gone into the jungle and retrieved the bolo that had wrapped itself around the trunk of a tree, cutting deeply into the bark. It was a weapon designed to cut off an arm or leg or head. Bits of glass had been glued to the bolo so that the string between the weights could cut deeply. She returned with it, unable to remain silent.

"This is a South American weapon. They shouldn't have it."

Tynan thought about responding, but decided again to ignore her. She would quickly realize that for modern men to have the weapons they had was not unusal. Travel through the region was no longer the life adventure it once had been. That these people had contact with the outside world was not strange. What was strange was that they could hide themselves so well. If she couldn't think of that

herself, Tynan wasn't interested in telling her. He just
wanted to get the hell out of the clearing before more of
the Mayans showed up.

Finally Jacobs approached and said, "I think that's got
it. We're ready."

"Then let's get out of here. Hernandez on point?"

"Right."

The SEAL took off, trotting across the jungle, looking
for the place where the Mayans had exited. He found it,
stopped, and studied the markings in the dew-wet grass
and the soft dirt. Finally he pushed into the vegetation.

Jacobs was right behind him, his weapon held at the
ready. Tynan walked with King, staying close to her,
while Lancer brought up the rear. Jefferson would stay
behind for an hour or so, or until both the wounded men
died. Then he would catch up. Lancer was responsible for
marking the trail so that Jefferson could follow.

Hernandez kept the pace slow. He crouched frequently,
touched the ground or the plants, and then looked off into
the distance. He would stand, turn, and then move off
again. He worked his way around the large trunks of the
giant trees, followed a path for a while, and then slipped
into the thick jungle vegetation.

And even though the pace was slow, Tynan found himself laboring before long. The humidity, as it did in most
rain forests, hugged the ground, oppressing everyone. As
the sun rose higher, the shade created by the interwoven
branches of the canopy worked like a greenhouse. The
heat seeped in, but didn't escape.

Tynan kept moving, wiping his face frequently. His
shirt was soon soaked with sweat and his face was flushed.
He felt like he was on fire and found his mind wandering.
Most the time he was concentrating on imagining an ice-
cold beer.

He glanced at King. She was in worse shape. Her khaki
shirt was as wet as it would have been if she had worn it in
a shower. The waistband of her skirt was wet. Her hair

hung down along her face, which was covered with sweat. Her color wasn't good and her mouth hung open as she sucked in the air.

"Jacobs," called Tynan. "Let's take a break."

Jacobs passed the order forward, and Hernandez stopped in his tracks. He scanned the jungle around him and then slipped to the rear. He knelt near Tynan and said, "We're on the right track. I don't think there's anyone out there in front of us though."

"We're alone?"

"Right now."

Tynan nodded and watched as King tipped her canteen to her lips. "Not too much," he cautioned her. "Sip it." He turned his attention to Hernandez. "What makes you think that we're alone in here?"

"The animals. They're all over the place. As we move toward them, we spook them, but they're there, to be spooked."

"You'll let me know if that changes?"

"Aye, aye, Skipper."

As Hernandez returned to his point position, Tynan took another look at King. "You going to be all right?"

"It's hot, that's all. Didn't expect it to be this hot with all this shade."

"It's the humidity," said Tynan. "In the Navy we have something called the wet bulb reading. Factors in the temperature with the relative humidity and tells us how uncomfortable it is. After a certain point, we cancel training and heavy activity because people are more prone to heat exhaustion."

"I'll be okay," she snapped. "If it only wasn't so damned hot."

"Tell you what," said Tynan. "Get yourself a rag and pour some water on it and then drape it around your neck. I know that it doesn't sound like much, but it helps. And pour a little water inside your helmet. That helps too."

Tynan stood then and worked his way around the tiny

perimeter. He'd given no orders for the increased security, but the SEALS knew what they were doing. They knew that if they could be attacked once, it could happen again, and they wanted to be ready.

He found Jefferson crouched at the base of a huge tree that was wrapped in clinging vines. The black man looked like he'd been swimming.

"The wounded men expired?"

"Yes, sir, not long after we left. Both of them died quickly, without a great deal of extra pain."

Tynan wasn't sure whether Jefferson was telling him that he'd killed the wounded men or if they had died naturally. Not that it really mattered, because the result was the same. He didn't want to ask, however.

Instead he said, "You have much trouble finding us?"

"No, sir. Lancer leaves real good signs. When I got close, it was easy to hear you."

"Yeah," agreed Tynan. "The noise discipline on this patrol is lousy, but that's mostly King's fault. She's not real good in the jungle."

"How long we going to stay here?"

"Couple more minutes. You looking for more rest?"

"No, sir. I just don't like it in the jungle. I prefer to be somewhere I can see what's going on around me."

"I hear that," said Tynan. He moved off then, heading back to where King rested. She had a rag around her neck. Her color was better.

"How you doing, Stevie?"

"Better," she said. She looked at him and added, "I want to say something here. I'm sorry about this morning. I didn't realize they would attack."

"Well," said Tynan, crouching down next to her, facing her. "You can't be blamed. In your world, everything is the ideal. You don't have much contact with violent people. In my world, I'm suspicious of everyone."

"I don't like that attitude," she said.

"I know what you mean, but there are people in this

world who would take advantage—hell, *do* take advantage of people like you. In your world, everyone operates on a higher level. They search for knowledge because the knowledge is good. In mine, too many of the people operate out of self-interest.''

"My world isn't that perfect," she said. "People steal theories, ideas, papers and present them as their own."

"But in the final analysis, no one is hurt. No one is left dead on the field."

"True," she said. "Is there a point to this?"

Tynan grinned. "You started it. I merely said that you didn't have to apologize for not understanding how the real world works."

"But I'm partly responsible for those men dying this morning. If I hadn't made that silly grandstand play . . ."

"If it hadn't been that, it would have been something else. Those men were looking to kill us. They knew we were around and they would have searched for us. This way, we had the upper hand."

"Still—"

"Look, this isn't the time or the place to get into a discussion of philosophy. If you're feeling up to it, we should hit the trail again."

He stood and turned. Hernandez was looking toward him and Tynan motioned him forward. Hernandez started again, following the trail that the Mayans had left.

Tynan helped King to her feet. He pointed to Hernandez and asked, "Is he heading toward that lost city of yours?"

"More or less, I think."

Tynan started out then, thinking. They could continue on, maybe walking into an ambush, if the Mayans were smart enough to set an ambush, or they could take a different route. One over terrain that was a little rougher. A route that men who had no reason to fear other men would never take. Not the easy route, but the hard one.

They stayed at it for an hour. They crossed one shallow stream. The water wasn't cold, but it was refreshing. King sat down in the middle of it, letting the water soak her thoroughly. She leaned back, closing her eyes, and let it wash over her head and face. When she stood up, her clothes molded themselves to her body, but she didn't care.

After the break at the stream, they moved faster. Hernandez stayed on point, checking the signs. They stayed at it until noon when Tynan called another halt. He figured they were far enough from the clearing that no one would be able to find them easily, and besides, they all needed a break.

Once security was set, he took out his map and examined it carefully. They had been traveling to the northeast, climbing steadily upward into the mountains. They had skirted one ridge that bordered a shallow valley. Through the center of the valley, visible in the sparkling of reflected sunlight, was a narrow river.

King had taken one look and said, "Copán was built in an area just like that. Fertile soil on an alluvial plain that could support the agriculture needed by the inhabitants of the city."

"But Copán isn't down there?"

"Copán should be due west of us. We're not that close to it here."

They finally came down off the ridge and started up another. When they reached the top, they stopped for a late lunch. Tynan ate his quickly. Then he moved closer to King and asked, "How much farther?"

She put the can she held on the ground and said, "Let me see your map." She pointed: "The lost city should be somewhere around here."

"No more than fifteen clicks."

"Providing we've got it spotted right," she said.

Hernandez approached them and leaned close to Tynan. "Skipper, I think someone is coming."

"You get a look at them?"

"Just heard them."

"Pass the word. Let's just fade into the jungle and wait to see who they are."

"Aye, aye." Hernandez moved off to warn the others.

"I take it that I can count on your cooperation on this one?"

"I'll be quiet."

"Okay." He helped her up and moved her away from the narrow, ill-defined trail. She slipped under a huge bush and promised not to move.

Tynan found cover near her, afraid that she would again feel the urge to contact whoever was walking around out there. He waited a moment to make sure that everyone else was hidden. To the right he could just make out the shape of Jacobs and to the left was Lancer. After they were hidden, Tynan took his place.

That done, all they could do was wait. Thirty minutes passed, and Tynan began to wonder if the people that Hernandez had heard had changed directions. This was the one thing that he didn't like—the waiting. He had no idea what they were facng and what would happen. He could have let his mind run wild: pictures of thousands of Mayan warriors swarming up the sides of the valley.

He forced himself to relax, listening for the approaching men. He finally heard something faint in the distance. He slowly turned his head and let his eyes search the bright green of the surrounding jungle. A bird broke cover, squawking its fright or anger, and then wheeled away.

Moments later the first of the Mayans stepped into view. It was like Tynan had again entered a time warp. These were warriors who weren't supposed to exist. They were something that was supposed to have vanished when the Spanish marched through, destroying the civilizations they found.

Now the men, dressed in the brightly colored togas, protected by leather padding and leather helmets and carrying spears topped with points made of stone or flint, wormed their way closer. Some held machetes that had obviously been made in modern factories. Others carried goatskins filled with water while a few had canteens. One of them even had a molded green plastic one that was becoming the standard issue of the U.S. military.

They moved closer, not maintaining any kind of a military formation. They talked with one another, their voices quiet. One stopped and took a drink and then hurried forward to catch up. They walked past quickly, not bothering to look right or left, and in ten minutes were out of sight.

When they were gone, Tynan slipped close to King and asked, "Well?"

"Just like the others. These people shouldn't exist in the modern world. This is a find of staggering proportions," she said. She shook head. "It's absolutely incredible."

"Then they're Mayan?"

"I think there's no doubt about it."

"They couldn't be villagers dressing up for some kind of ritual or celebration?"

King looked at him and said, "I suppose that could be the case, but still . . ."

"Okay," said Tynan. He moved toward Hernandez and took out his map. "I think that it's time we altered our path." He pointed to the spot marked on his map and said, "This is our destination."

Hernandez looked at the map and then the terrain. "We go down here, and then across the valley floor, that should get us there."

"If it's a more direct route," said Tynan, "I wonder why these people don't use it."

"Terrain could be rougher. Could be that this path takes them somewhere else they want to go." Hernandez shrugged. "Who knows?"

"Let's do it then," said Tynan.

Hernandez took a compass reading and started off again. He changed direction once and faded into the jungle.

Jacobs followed as before. Lancer and Jefferson brought
up the rear.

The climb down was awkward; the slope steepened,
making it hard to walk. They slipped frequently, sometimes sliding several feet before stopping. They made
noise, but that couldn't be helped. Tynan also realized
why the Mayans followed the trail. It might be shorter to
go straight down the hillside, but it wasn't very easy.
Climbing up it would have been hot, tiring work, while
following the path was relatively easy.

At the bottom of the slope they stopped again. Now they
were covered with dirt as well as sweat. Tynan was breathing hard. His muscles ached from the strain. He stood,
moved to a tall tree, and put a hand on it. He stared across
the valley floor and saw that the other side was just as
steep.

"Skipper, Hernandez says that we're no more than half
a click from the trail, if he remembers the map right," said
Jacobs.

Tynan turned and looked in that direction, but the vegetation was too thick for him to see anything. He wiped the
sweat from his face and asked, "You think we can main-
tain the noise discipline necessary to give us warning that
someone else is coming?"

"No problem from my people. Your Dr. King is the one
we have to worry about."

She looked up from where she lay on the jungle floor.
"Just pretend that I don't exist."

"Give Hernandez a big enough lead and that won't be a
problem," said Tynan.

"He deserves a break from point," said Jacobs. "He's
been on it all day."

"Fine, detail someone else or take it yourself. I'll want
someone good in the slack position too. I want us strung
out pretty good so that we don't get caught."

"These guys aren't going to ambush us," said Jacobs.

Tynan shrugged. "I don't think so either, but I don't want to get fooled."

"How soon?"

Tynan looked down at King. Her breathing had slowed and her color was good. She looked tired, but not sick, as she had in the morning.

"Give us twenty minutes to relax and cool off. Signal me when you're ready."

Jacobs turned and left, heading toward the path. As he disappeared into the jungle, King said, "Am I really that much of a burden?"

"Well," said Tynan, "honestly, you're not very good in the jungle. Don't understand the environment."

"That all?"

"Listen, when we get out of here, we'll sit down over a cold beer and I'll tell you what you need to learn about the jungle. Show you what you've done wrong. Now, all you have to remember is to move as quietly as you can but don't get so hung up on not making noise that you're afraid to move."

"Thanks."

Tynan sat down and took a drink from his canteen. Not the refreshing cold water that he wished he had, but sun warm water that tasted of plastic and purification tablets. He was afraid of the water in the stream nearby because he didn't know what happened in the hills above him. Everyone had the habit of taking water upstream and dumping garbage and sewage in it downstream. It was safer drinking the water he had carried in, although in another day he would be out of it.

Jacobs returned then and held up a hand. Tynan nodded and got to his feet. "That's it. We're taking off again."

King didn't move. She opened her eyes and said, "Could you just come back for my body later?"

"Could, but won't. We might find an easier way out, so if you don't get up, you can just stay here."

She struggled to sit up and then slowly climbed to her feet. "No rest for the weary."

"It's your party we're going to."

She nodded but didn't speak.

Together they moved forward and then fell into line with the others. Tynan could catch glimpses of Jacobs and Hernandez through the trees and bushes. They were on the path ahead of him, climbing up the hill. The trail wasn't much more than a narrow path worn in the vegetation. It switched back and forth so that the angle of the climb wasn't too great. Designed just like the roads through the Rocky Mountains.

The sun dipped toward the horizon and it seemed to get cooler in the jungle. Tynan found himself enjoying the walk. It wasn't anything like the central highlands in Vietnam where an enemy ambush could spring at any moment. Or, if that didn't happen, he could step on a booby trap that could end his sex life or his Navy career. He could end up in a body bag. There wasn't that kind of pressure here. All he had to do was try to avoid the poisonous snakes, which normally made a habit of avoiding him.

He felt the urge to run. Hurry up the hill, where he was sure they would camp for the night. They'd made good progress and the last thing he wanted was to find this lost city just as the light faded. If King was right and there were people there, he wanted as much daylight as possible when they arrived. The morning would be better.

And then the urge to run turned into a desire to flee: as they approached the top of the ridge, the drums started again. This time they weren't distant things just barely audible. They were loud, hammering things that filled the jungle with noise, a pounding beat that seemed to vibrate through the ground and shake the vegetation.

"What is that?" Tynan demanded of King.

"I would say that someone has figured out that the men who attacked us this morning aren't coming back."

He stared at her. "But they haven't had time to get there and back. There is no way they can know."

"Unless the failure of the raiding party to return has told them. I would guess that a larger party, armed with more and better weapons, will be sent."

Tynan stopped and demanded, "When?"

"Probably not until after sundown. They'll need a couple of hours to prepare."

"Okay," said Tynan. "Gives us time to get off the trail and let the party walk past us."

"Providing they haven't spotted us already."

Tynan felt the blood drain from his face. He wiped a hand over his forehead and said, "Do you know something that you had better share with me?"

"No. No, I'm just guessing. They'd have guards out, but they might not have spotted us."

Tynan started to move again and then saw that Hernandez had stopped moving. He hurried forward and leaned close to the SEAL. "What is it?"

Hernandez shrugged and pointed to where Jacobs crouched at the side of the trail. Tynan hesitated, waiting for the pointman to either move or to signal him, but that didn't happen. Jacobs kept facing forward, watching something.

Tynan crept forward, keeping low. As he approached, Jacobs glanced at him and Tynan raised his eyebrows in question.

Jacobs shrugged and then pointed. When Tynan was close, Jacobs whispered, "I think we've arrived."

10

The dripping of the water was becoming irritating. A constant noise. Moore sat with his back to the wall, listening to the water drip, concentrating on it because no matter how bad it was, it was better than the sound of tiny claws on the stone. Scrambling claws. But with so little light, with no light, Moore didn't know if they were rats or lizards.

Sara stood up most the time, in the center of the cell. She whimpered occasionally, ignoring everything that either he or Jason Hughes said. She was afraid of the rats, remembering stories of them attacking children, ripping at adults who couldn't defend themselves, killing small animals with their razor-sharp teeth.

It was a brilliant bit of psychological warfare: Take a person's sight from him and fill the dark with noises. Let the imagination run wild. If they could see the rats or the lizards, the horror would be reduced.

Moore stood up and again felt his way around the cell; again he found nothing that would help him escape. It wouldn't be so bad, he thought, if he had no idea of his fate. But he knew what it was. The Mayans, at the end of their civilization, went through a period of human sacrifice. Thousands were killed and Moore knew that was what would happen to him and the others.

Hughes, standing near the stone that blocked the entrance, said, "Maybe we could rush them when they open the door." He spoke quietly, but his voice echoed in the chamber, making it sound larger than it was.

"Rush them," said Moore. "And then what? Take their swords and kill them?"

"Better them than us," said Hughes.

Moore didn't have an answer to that one because he believed it, too. Instead he said, "Jason, you know anything about fighting? Have you ever been in a fight?"

Hughes shrugged but the gesture was lost in the dark. "Grade school."

"And you're going to overpower trained guards?"

"Who said they've been trained? Maybe they were just pulled off the street and told to guard us."

"Okay," said Moore. "Suppose that's the case. But they're carrying weapons they know how to use. You ever held a sword in your hand? Ever been in a knife fight?"

"So what are you suggesting?" demanded Hughes.

"That we don't go off half-cocked. We've got to think our way through this. Use our brains to get out of here, because we'll lose if we try to fight our way out."

Sara said, "We have to get out of here." Her voice was shakey, as if she were on the verge of hysteria.

"We will," said Moore. "We just have to put our minds on it. We'll think of something."

Tynan crawled through the dense grass and peeked over the top of the ridge. Spread out below him, shielded from the air by a thick canopy of interwoven leaves and branches of the tallest trees and an overhanging cliff, was the Mayan city that King had told him about. The city was situated the farthest south in the Mayan empire, beating out Copán by fifty or sixty miles. A city that, like Copán, was erected on an alluvial plain, but one that was a smaller version, no more than a square mile in area. It was a city that Tynan had thought didn't exist.

There were the classic pyramids with the smaller buildings surrounding them. To one side was an open field that
looked like a football stadium made of stone and that had a
grass field. There were paved streets and there were people
circulating down there. No more than a hundred of them,
working their way through a market area of wooden stalls.
There was a single fire burning behind one stall as if it
were the fast-food restaurant stuck in the middle of a mall.

Tynan pulled out his binoculars and examined the city
closely. It was not the ruin that he had expected. He had
thought that it would be a crumbling city with inhabitants
living in thatched structures build on the decaying pyramids. Instead, it was a functioning city that had been kept
up. No ruins here. These were new, inhabited buildings.

He leaned closer to Jacobs and said, "I don't suppose
that you've seen the missing people."

"No," he responded, his voice quiet, almost unintelligible. "But then, they'd be locked up somewhere."

"Great," said Tynan.

"What do we do now, Skipper?"

Tynan raised the binoculars and scanned the city. Men,
women, and childen walked around. More people were
sitting outside, working at various tasks. One man was
carving jade. Another was scraping the inside of a hide. A
woman hammered at a small sheet of gold with a stone,
and another was working to make a clay pot.

He turned and glanced to the rear. He could see King
kneeling at the side of the path, but the others were
invisible, having taken up security positions. Tynan waited
for King to look at him, and then waved her forward. As
she approached, he motioned for her to get down, finally
signaling for her to crawl the last few feet.

She reached them, and then looked over the top of the
ridge. She gasped once. "Good God. It's a living city."

"If your friends are alive, they'll be down there," said
Tynan quietly.

"Yes," agreed King, nodding. "Assuming that we were

right about their being captured, they would have been brought here.''

''Do you know where they would be?''

She was silent for a moment and then said, ''My guess is they would be held under the main pyramid or in a building close to it. Sacrificial victims would be kept there.''

''How many people would live in that city?''

''Well, some of the ceremonial centers contained as many as a hundred thousand residents. The Aztec city of Tenochtitlán may have reached a population of over one million, but that was a much larger area.'' She fell silent and then added, ''I wouldn't expect more than five thousand people down there.''

''Christ,'' said Jacobs.

''That complicates this somewhat,'' said Tynan. ''There is no way we can get in there with that many people around.''

''You have to remember that only a few of the people will be soldiers. Most are craftsmen or farmers who will be inside during the night. The streets will remain vacant.''

''What about the drums?'' asked Tynan.

''Those are arranged on the top of the pyramid, hidden in that temple on top. We don't have to worry about that.''

Tynan slipped to the right then and used his binoculars. The city had been built with an eye to using the jungle to conceal it from anyone approaching. Maybe it was the result of the Spanish conquests of the Aztec and Inca. Maybe it was a result of the Spanish enslavement of the Indian populations as they hunted for riches in the new world. Whatever the reason, the builders had used the jungle and, by doing that, allowed Tynan and his men the opportunity to sneak to the edge of the city.

The cliffs behind the city, with the overhang of the mountains, made that approach impossible for them. Under other circumstances, with the proper equipment, it was the approach that he would have used, but not this time.

The trail wound down the hillside to the south of where he was. He could see a short portion of it. At the foot of the hill, near where the trail left the jungle and became a stone-paved road, was a hut where guards stood. Their function might be nothing more than ceremonial, but there was no reason to use the path.

A stream dropped over a short cliff and then wormed down the hill until it passed through the center of the city. It widened there, and there were bridges constructed across it. The Mayans had paved the riverbed with stone and Tynan was reminded of the Los Angeles River in the United States—a paved route for the water that had become the set of a hundred movies.

The cover near the river was the best. It also put them at the edge of the city closest to the pyramid where King thought the missing people were being held.

King whispered, "Are you going to go down there?"

"Not until after dark. Right now I'm going to study the layout of the city so that I'll be able to find my way around when I get there."

He slipped closer to Jacobs and handed him the binoculars. "I think we need to shift our base about three hundred meters to the left. Set up near the stream and then work our way into the city."

Jacobs put the binoculars to his eyes and scanned the scene. He finally nodded. "There's a route down on the other side of the valley." He pointed to a place where the overhang retreated into the side of the mountain. It would be a hard climb but one that would put them at the foot of the pyramid, out of sight of anyone in the city proper.

"Take us a day to get into position over there. There are too many people around. We've got to go tonight. If we wait, someone is liable to stumble over us."

Tynan took the binoculars back and returned them to their case. He slipped to the rear, away from the top of the ridge line, and waited. Jacobs joined him quickly. When

King arrived, they worked their way back to where the others waited.

Again Jacobs took point. Now they moved with exaggerated caution. Each man made sure that he wouldn't snap a twig or rustle leaves of the bushes. King followed in Tynan's footsteps, aware of his criticism of her.

It took them an hour to reach the stream. They crossed it carefully, not wanting to stir up the silt on the bottom because that might tell someone downstream that they were there.

Jacobs found the perfect hiding place. He crawled under the flowing branches of a large bush until he reached a huge rock outcropping. There was a depression in it where they could store the gear they wouldn't take into the valley. If something went wrong, searchers might overlook the site so that Tynan and his men could retrieve the equipment later. And given the fall of the land, if they took out the bush, they would have a defensible position.

They slid into place, posting Jefferson and Lancer as the first guards. Once inside, Tynan and Jacobs slipped their packs from their shoulders. Hernandez checked out the depression before following suit. King dropped to the ground, relaxing for the first time since they had left the camp that morning.

Tynan felt like he was going to float upward with the weight removed from his back. He unconsciously kept a hand wrapped around his equipment, as if holding himself on the ground. He sipped his water and felt better.

They sat quietly as the sun set and the ground was bathed in darkness. Far below them, through gaps in the foliage, they could see flickering lights as Mayans using torches and fat lamps moved through their city. But the lights were never in one place long, nor were they very bright. It was almost as if they had a blackout regulation designed to thwart aerial recon. A large source of light would eventually turn up on a satellite photo and invite investigation. In fact, that was almost what had happened.

If it hadn't been for the infrared mapping of Central America, the site would still be unknown.

While they waited for the city to settle down, the drums kept at it, a constant reminder that there was danger around them. Tynan became uneasy again. As noisy as those drums were, it would have seemed that someone would have investigated them earlier. How could this have remained hidden from the outside world for so long? None of it was comforting, because it also suggested that if anyone had indeed investigated the drums, they had obviously failed to return with a report.

Tynan took his turn at guard. He shifted around so that he could watch the activity in the city. At first it seemed that many people were about. As time passed, the lights became fewer and he knew that everything was settling down. Given what he knew of human psychology, he knew that the best time for the recon would be after midnight. It would take them an hour or more to get down there. If they entered the city about two, everyone would be at the lowest ebb, people would be in the deepest sleep, and a minor mistake might not prove fatal.

Finally he returned to the camp and touched Jacobs on the shoulder. He leaned close and whispered, "It's time."

Jacobs sat up and nodded. He rolled off his sleeping bag and woke Hernandez and Lancer. While Jefferson, who had been on guard with him, checked the equipment, Tynan woke King. She came awake by going rigid, as if frightened, but made no sound.

Before he moved into the bush, Jacobs leaned close and asked, "What happens if we run into someone?"

This was the question that Tynan had been thinking about for the last few hours. If they ran into a man armed with a spear, the answer was simple. They'd kill him. But what if it was a woman or a kid? He couldn't order the men to kill them.

"If it's a man, kill him. If it's a woman or a kid, we'll

take them prisoner, releasing them once we're out of the city.''

"And if we run into more than one?"

"We'll cross that bridge when we come to it. We've got to remember that this is not Vietnam and these people aren't really the enemy."

But even as he said it, he knew it wasn't true. These people *were* the enemy, if only until he could get out of their valley. They would kill quickly, without hesitation, and by putting restrictions on his own men he was giving the enemy the advantage. It was the muddled thinking that he cursed when he was in Vietnam. Politicians who thought it was fine to bomb military installations but who screamed when the bombs fell short or long and innocents were killed. Politicians who dictated that certain areas of Vietnam were free fire zones where anything that moved was to be shot and then complained when the victims of that policy turned out to be women and children.

Before Jacobs moved, Tynan whispered. "Let the men know that however they feel they have to handle the situation is fine. Let's try to avoid killing people, but if it can't be helped, then it can't be helped."

"Aye, aye, sir."

King came forward and asked, "What do you want me to do?"

"Ideally, we'd leave you here, but if the missing people aren't where you think they should be, we'll need another guess and you can't help us if you're up here."

"Okay."

Tynan turned, found Jefferson and said, "I want you to stay close to Dr. King. We get into trouble, you get her out. You don't worry about us."

"Yes, sir."

"And hang back so that you won't get picked up with us if something goes wrong."

Jefferson nodded.

Before they moved out, Tynan went through the equipment packs. There were many things that they wouldn't need during the recon—entrenching tools, the spare radio batteries, extra food, and extra canteens. Other things might prove useful, such as flashlights. Tynan didn't want to weigh the men down with equipment they wouldn't use, but then, there was always the possibility that the situation would develop so that they couldn't get back. It was a risk leaving the equipment, but given the whole situation, it was one that Tynan would take. Replacement equipment wasn't that far away.

Once the men had the necessary equipment, Tynan moved forward to where Jacobs waited. He touched the big man on the shoulder and said, "Let's do it."

Jacobs moved out, skirting the bank of the stream. He dodged once deeper into the jungle and then broke out again. He kept the pace slow as he worked his way down toward the city.

As they neared it, they could hear sounds from it, sounds that penetrated through the rhythmic hammering of the drums: cries in the night; children calling to parents; a few shouts; the barking of a dog.

And, of course, the drums.

When Jacobs reached the edge of the city, he stopped. Tynan caught up to him and crouched near him. Jacobs looked once at the SEAL commander and then entered into the city. He moved along one stone street, his back against the walls of the buildings.

Tynan followed, keeping his eyes open for trouble. As they neared the central pyramid, he noticed that many of the buildings were vacant. They weren't made of stone, but an adobelike brick with thatching for the roof.

They moved on, the patrol stringing out along the street. Jacobs turned toward the main pyramid and stopped. He crouched, and when Tynan looked, he pointed to the top.

Now they could see a flickering of light there. The drumming had become thunderous, drowning out all other sound. People, dressed in white, were moving about the top.

Tynan worked his way closer to Jacobs and studied the pyramid. From the little he remembered from college anthro courses, he had the impression that Central American pyramids were little more than stone-covered rubble heaps. They were not the elaborate structures that had been built in Eygpt.

There were steps leading toward the top. Stone carvings covered the surface of the pyramid, but there didn't seem to be any doorways that would lead inside where King claimed the prisoners, if there were prisoners, would be held.

Tynan signaled Jacobs to hold where he was. Then Tynan slipped to the rear. He found King and pulled her to the side. "You sure that the cells are under the pyramid?"

"Not directly under it. There'll be buildings to the sides with tunnels leading into the pyramid and to the temple on the top."

"How do we find those?"

"You'll just have to look for them."

Tynan wanted to hit her. Instead, he made his way back to Jacobs and leaned close.

"We'll need to search the area at the base of the pyramid. There should be some buildings there that'll lead us down into the dungeon area."

Jacobs nodded and moved forward. He veered away from the pyramid, heading for the single-story buildings that surrounded it. He stopped near the entrance to one, surprised that there was no door. A curtain closed it off. He listened, but there was no sound from the interior. He stepped inside and waited.

Tynan joined him after signaling the others to wait. The interior was pitch black. No shades of gray or light. Just a smooth blackness. Tynan reached to his harness and pulled his flashlight free. He cupped his fingers over the lens and turned it on.

The dim beam stabbed out, showing that the room was nearly bare. He turned slowly and then jumped as the beam swept over a figure lying on a cot. But there was no movement in the figure and the dusky smell rising from everywhere suggested that no one lived in the house. He turned the flashlight beam on the prone form and realized that it was a dead man—dead for a long time, the skin dried and mummified, the body wrapped in dirty rags.

"What the fuck?" whispered Jacobs.

"I don't know," said Tynan. "Let's get out of here."

As they reappeared, King moved closer, Jefferson right behind her. Before either man could speak, King said, "That's someone's house. No way down in it."

"The occupant is dead," Tynan said.

"Of course. When the owner dies, the family and relatives move out, usually burying the body under the floor."

"This guy was lying on a cot."

"Then he was an important man. Maybe a ruler. Maybe a priest."

Tynan realized that the last thing he needed was a lecture on Mayan death customs. To King, he said, "Is there some way to tell the residences from the structures we need?"

"Look for a stone building with a wooden door."

"Jacobs?"

"Got it, Skipper."

"Then, let's go."

Again Jacobs started off. He passed a number of buildings until he stopped at one. Tynan caught him, saw that it was made of stone, and said, "Go."

Jacobs stepped to the door and reached for the knob, but there wasn't one. He found the latch and lifted it, swinging the door inward, waiting for the creak of the hinges, but there wasn't a sound. He glanced right and left and stepped inside.

Tynan, his rifle held at the ready, followed. He found Jacobs crouched at the far end of the room, looking down a flight of stone steps. A dim flickering came from the lower level.

Tynan turned and waved the other men forward. When they were inside, he said, "I want Jefferson and Lancer to wait here, cover the rear. Hernandez, you'll go with us."

"Aye, aye, sir."

"Go, Jacobs," said Tynan.

The big man took a step down and froze. He leaned back against the rough-hewn stone wall. He looked up toward Tynan, and then started down again.

When Jacobs was halfway to the doorway at the bottom of the stairs, Tynan began to follow. As soon as he put a foot on the first riser, he realized that the steps were steeper than those he was used to.

Jacobs stopped at the doorway and let Tynan catch up. The doorway opened on a long hallway lined with stone. There were torches and fat lamps attached to the walls which had moss growing on them. There was a drip of water from somewhere. Voices bubbled up from a lower level.

"Go ahead," said Tynan.

Jacobs moved again, entering the corridor. He stopped at the first door and looked into what was apparently an empty cell. Tynan came forward, moving along the wall on the other side of the corridor. He felt a cool wind blowing up from somewhere, carrying the stench of dirty people.

Tynan slipped into the lead, glancing into the empty cells as they passed them. He stopped once, entered a cell, and then returned to the main corridor. He glanced back and saw Hernandez backing them up. The SEAL was watching their rear as if he expected the Mayans to suddenly appear behind them.

They came to a branch in the corridor. One side descended into darkness. The other was lighted and looked as if it was a carbon copy of the one they had just come through.

"Skipper?"

Tynan shrugged, not knowing which way. "Take the dark one."

Jacobs jerked his light from his belt and switched it on. He flashed it around. The corridor had a slight slant to it. He entered it, waited for Tynan, and then began to move.

As Tynan entered, he wiped his face with the back of his hand. He could feel the tension in his muscles. At any moment they could be discovered, someone could pop out of the darkness and shout the alarm. Tynan was convinced they could shoot their way out of any trouble, but that was the last thing he wanted.

He followed Jacobs until he reached a bend in the corridor. The man stopped and waited for Tynan.

Tynan approached carefully, and then crouched, letting Jacobs use his light to illuminate the corridor. He studied it and then said, "Unless I miss my guess, it's bending back the way we came."

"Yes, sir."

"Okay, then let's follow it for a while. You haven't seen a way to get any lower have you?"

"Each of the cells was empty. There didn't seem to be a stairway in any of them."

"Yeah," said Tynan. "I wouldn't think that they would spend too much effort in tunneling."

But then he remembered the Vietcong had wasted a great deal of time tunneling. Decades spent lacing South Vietnam with tunnels so that they could move around underground without having to worry about the Americans and South Vietnamese above them. It wasn't as if the Mayans here didn't have the same incentive—a reason to avoid contact with the outside world. That bothered Tynan, but he kept the thoughts to himself.

They were halfway down the corridor when they came to the only sealed cell. There was a large round stone pushed up against the wall and although there was no evidence of a door behind it, there had to be one there.

Jacobs played his flashlight over it. "What do you think?"

Tynan leaned against it, shoved, and then said, "Help me push."

Together then shifted it slightly. Tynan stood up and the stone rocked back into a slight groove. He slung his rifle and leaned a shoulder against it. Jacobs did the same.

"On three," said Tynan. "One. Two. *Three*."

He grunted with the effort, but the stone rolled. He pushed hard to keep it going until it revealed the doorway that had been behind it.

"Shine the light in here."

Jacobs held the light at arm's length, the way police officers did, so that they wouldn't be targets. He saw movement on the inside of the cell. He flipped the light toward it and said, "I think we've found them."

There was a moment of silence from inside the cell and then a voice boomed at them: "My God! You're Americans."

11

It seemed too easy. They had slipped into the city, located the undergound cells and then found the missing people. All quickly and without any trouble. Tynan was afraid of a mission that worked that well. He hated it when everything came together so easily, because it meant that total disaster was around the next corner.

There was a moment when everyone stood there stunned. No one moved and then Moore burst from his cell, blinking in the brightness of the flashlight. He held out a hand, grabbing at Tynan. "I'm Dr. Moore. Brian Moore. I'm glad to see you."

Tynan tried to separate himself from Moore, pushing the man to the side. "Are there others with you?"

Moore moved to Jacobs but Jacobs held his weapon in one hand and his flashlight in the other. Moore patted him on the shoulder and said, "Thank you. Thank you. I knew someone would come."

"Please, Doctor," said Jacobs. "Quietly. Speak quietly."

Tynan moved into the cell and saw a shape huddled in one corner. He moved to it and reached out, touching it on the head. There was a piecing scream of pure panic. The body didn't move. Tynan knelt and tried to see into the eyes.

"You're going to be fine," he said. "Just fine. We've come to get you out."

There was a voice behind him then. "Who are you?"

Tynan glanced back but saw only the dimmest outline in the dark. "Tynan. United States Navy."

"Navy? What in the hell are you doing here?"

"Came to get you out. We've got to move."

The man came out of the darkness and reached past Tynan. He lifted the girl to her feet. "We're free, Sara."

The woman seemed to suddenly understand. She sobbed once and threw herself at Tynan, hugging him tightly. She kissed his neck and cheek, breathing, "Thank you, thank you," over and over.

Tynan guided her out of the cell. "We're going to have to get out of here now."

Moore didn't move. He said, "There are others from our party down here."

"Shit!" said Jacobs.

"Do you know where they are?" asked Tynan.

"No," said Moore. "We were separated when we were brought in."

Tynan rubbed his face with his fingers. He wanted to throw up his hands because he had run out of ideas. He glanced down the corridor, but there were no other sealed cells. The others could be around a corner, on a different level, or in a different place altogether. As he stood there, his mind racing, he was aware of the time slipping by.

"Okay. Hernandez, take these people back to the surface and leave them upstairs with Lancer and Jefferson."

"Skipper," said Jacobs.

"I know. We're dividing our forces in hostile territory without a clue about the enemy."

"Hernandez, get these people out of here."

"Aye, aye."

Tynan pointed down the corridor. "Let's get going."

Jacobs stood for a moment, staring into Tynan's face,

and then turned. He started down the corridor, his flashlight bouncing from wall to wall.

Tynan slipped along the other side, as he had done earlier. He kept his eyes open, but didn't see anything that would give him a clue about the others. When they came to a corner, both stopped, Tynan kneeling near the wall.

A piercing scream cut through the air. There was a single shot and then a short burst. Four or five rounds fired on full auto.

"Skipper?" said Jacobs, his voice rising.

Again Tynan hesitated, wondering if there were others hidden in cells deeper in the dungeon. There was another shot and a scream that sounded like a man who had taken a round through the stomach.

Tynan nodded and pointed to the rear. "Okay. Let's not run headlong into trouble."

Jacobs snapped off his flashlight and hooked it on his web pistol belt. He worked the bolt of his weapon, ejecting a live round. He ignored the sound as the bullet hit the floor. Without a glance at Tynan, he started back up the corridor.

Tynan was right behind him. His thumb moved to the safety of his M16, flicking it to single shot. He didn't bother with the bolt, knowing that a round was chambered.

As they hurried back the way they had come, their ears strained for more sounds. There was a muffled grunt that surprised them and then silence. They reached the corner and halted there. Jacobs covered while Tynan looked around the corner.

It was darker than it had been. One fat lamp lay on the stone floor, the liquid from it spreading in a glowing, flaming stain. The torches had been pulled down and extinguished. Two other fat lamps continued to burn.

Hernandez and the others were about halfway along the corridor, or at least seemed to be. He could see Hernandez peeking out of a cell, searching the corridor. There were four bodies on the floor—two of them near Hernandez, one about halfway to the opposite side, and one near the stairway that would lead up.

Tynan snapped his fingers at Jacobs and pointed to the cell. Jacobs nodded and Tyan held up three fingers, then two and finally one. As he shot his index finger out, Jacobs moved.

Together they rushed toward the cell. Hernandez saw them coming and ducked inside. As Tynan got there, he said, "What happened?"

"Six of them appeared in the corridor in front of us, stunned that we were there. When the woman screamed, they rushed us. I shot once, hoping that the noise would frighten them, but they kept coming. I had to shoot to kill. They turned and ran toward the steps and I tried to stop that. Then they disappeared into a side passage or one of the cells. They didn't head up the stairs because there was no shooting from there."

"Okay," said Tynan. "We've got to get out of here. Maybe no one in the city heard the shots. Jacobs, take point and I'll bring up the rear. None of your people were hurt?"

"No, sir."

"Then, let's go."

Jacobs checked the corridor and took off, hurrying toward the stairs. Tynan waited until everyone was in the hallway, moving well, and then entered it himself. He kept glancing to the rear, hoping that the Mayans would stay hidden, frightened by the guns.

But before he could catch the others, four men leaped into the hallway. One of them held a torch over his head. He pointed to Tynan and shouted. The others, two holding spears and one with a machete, came at him. They hunched over, like men fighting a strong wind. They chattered among themselves.

Tynan whirled to face them. He held his M16 with the butt pressed against his hip. The men were not intimidated.

He raised the barrel and fired a single shot into the ceiling. The round whined off the stone with a ringing screech.

With that, the men attacked. Tynan took a step back and shot once as he swung his weapon down. The round took the warrior in the chest, flipping him to the rear. He hit the stone wall and slid to the floor without a sound. Blood gushed from the wound, spreading in a growing black stain.

But the others kept coming. Tynan fired again. One warrior stumbled but didn't fall. Blood blossomed on his shoulder and he dropped his spear, but he didn't fall.

The other spear carrier stopped and hurled his weapon. It hit the stone next to Tynan's head and the point shattered. He snatched the other spear from the floor and attacked.

The man with the machete was nearly on him then. He swung at Tynan's head, trying to chop it off. The SEAL ducked and kicked out. His boot shattered the knee of the warrior. The man dropped, screaming.

Now Tynan swung on the last of his attackers. He parried a thrust of the spear, shoving it toward the wall. The warrior danced back and came again. Tynan fired once. The round caught the man in the side of the head. The rear of his skull blew off in a shower of blood and brain. He dropped and then kicked out, his body spasming. He rolled over until he hit the walk and then flopped around like a chicken without a head.

Tynan leaped over the body of one of the Mayans and sprinted up the corridor. As he reached the steps, he saw Jacobs coming back down to help. Tynan waved at him, and the other man retreated rapidly.

When he reached the top of the steps, he could see Jefferson and Lancer crouched near the door, watching the streets outside them.

"We've got trouble," said Jacobs.

"That's obvious."

"There are more of them out there. Fifty or more, all

warriors. They've scattered now, taking cover at the sides
of the buildings and in doorways.''

"Damn it," snapped Tynan. "I didn't want this. I tried
to avoid a fight. King, what's happening?"

She moved out of the gloom. "They're going to attack.
They've got a ritual to perform and then they'll swarm out
of hiding, prepared to die."

Tynan glanced around the stone building. There were a
couple of windows and the stairway down. The corridors
led to the pyramid, according to King, which meant they'd
have to cover their rear too. But the building was defensible. With automatic weapons, a hundred men with only
spears and knives weren't much of a threat.

Tynan pointed to one of the windows and then at Lancer.
"Cover that." He assigned Hernandez the other window
and told Jefferson to check out the people they had rescued
and then watch the stairs. Then he and Jacobs took the
door, one man on either side of it.

As he took his position, the drumbeat increased, becoming faster and louder. There was movement on the top of
the pyramid. Lights seemed to swirl up there, flickering
and dancing and disappearing.

"King," yelled Tynan, "what's going on?"

Instead, Moore came forward and crouched next to Tynan.
"It would appear that they are getting ready for a sacrifice
and that we are going to be the guests of honor."

Tynan, his weapon pointed out the door, said, "I don't
understand this sacrifice thing. How can *we* be the sacrifice. They lose nothing by sacrificing us."

"I don't pretend to understand it," said Moore. "Apparently their gods don't care who dies as long as human
blood is spilled. Yours will do as nicely as anyone's."

"Great."

Movement to their front caught Tynan's attention. He
turned toward it, but the shapes vanished. There was
shouting from that quarter, but no one came at them yet.

Then, suddenly, the drums stopped. Tynan glanced at

Moore who shrugged. The lights at the top of the pyramid stopped moving and were placed at the very edge, lighting it almost as brightly as if it were daylight. A single man wearing a bloodred robe, his head covered with a feathered mask, came forward and began shouting.

"You understand him?" asked Tynan.

"No," said Moore. "The spoken language today is different." He realized that didn't sound right. He'd meant that the man on the pyramid was speaking an ancient dialect and not what the farmers in the region spoke.

"Skipper," said Lancer. "I have movement over here."

"Is it a problem?"

"Not yet. Just wanted you to know that they're moving on this side."

Tynan turned his attention back to the top of the pyramid. The man there pointed to the rear and someone was dragged forward.

"Christ, it's Jimmy," said Moore.

"One of your missing people?" Tynan asked.

But Moore didn't have to answer. The man wore khaki shorts and a white shirt. He stood stiffly as the priest in the robe pushed a knife to his throat. The priest continued to yell, his words coming in staccato bursts. Jim screamed once either in fear or pain, but didn't move.

The priest waved the knife once in air and then cut the man's throat. Blood, looking black in the flickering light, splashed over the front of his shirt. His knees sagged and as they did, the priest shoved the body out. Jim took one stumbling step and fell over the edge of the pyramid. He hit the side, bounced, and then slid to the ground.

"Christ," Moore said again.

The priest spun and vanished. He reappeared a moment later, this time with a woman. Like Jim, she was dressed in khaki shorts but she wore a khaki shirt. The sound of her crying drifted to them.

"I think I can take him, Skipper," said Jacobs.

"Then do it. Now!"

Jacobs pressed the side of his weapon against the door jam to steady it. He twisted around and leaned into the butt of the weapon. He said nothing, concentrating on the target. He squeezed the trigger, letting the weapon fire when ready.

The shot seemed to have missed the priest. But then he took a step to the rear. He dropped the ceremonial dagger and fell backward, disappearing. The woman began to scream then, her voice piercing through the dark.

Moore jumped to center of the door and shouted, "Run, Linda. Run."

But she didn't hear him. She let her panic consume her. She stood at the top of the pyramid, screaming, her hands at her sides. Another person appeared, but didn't stand there long. He plunged a knife into her chest and threw her over the edge of the pyramid. Before Jacobs could fire again, the man vanished.

And then the warriors who had been gathering at the base of the pyramid attacked. They roared down the streets, screaming, waving their swords and spears.

Tynan never gave the order to open fire. He aimed his weapon and shot. The man leading the attack fell. Those behind him leaped over the body and kept coming. Tynan pulled the trigger again and again. The muzzle flash stabbed out. Tracers bounced through the streets. More men fell, some screaming, and still the Mayans came.

The bolt of Tynan's weapon locked back. He twisted around, his back to the wall. He hit the magazine release and dropped it to the dirty stone floor. He slammed another one home and realized that he didn't have that much to spare. The last thing that he had expected was a firefight.

He turned again and aimed. The Mayans were closer now. The sound of firing filled the room around him. He could smell the cordite and hear the ejected brass hitting the the stone. One of the women was crying.

Ignoring that, Tynan fired. The Mayan warrior was

tossed to the side, hitting the stone wall. He fell and the man beind him tripped over him.

The drumming began again, accompanied by the sound of trumpets. The screaming from the attacking soldiers died down, and then the men seemed to vanish. They turned into doorways and side streets or turned and ran back the way they came.

"Skipper, we can't hold out here long."

Tynan didn't answer that. He checked his ammo and found that he had only three magazines for the M16 and two for his Browning. A full-out attack would burn through that in a matter of minutes and if the fight degenerated to hand to hand, Tynan knew they didn't have a chance.

"Jefferson, can everyone travel?"

"Everyone's fine."

Tynan nodded and glanced out the door. The streets were empty but that didn't mean much. There could be a thousand people hiding among the stone houses. He knew that the corridors below them were supposed to be connected to the pyramid and that might provide an avenue of escape, but he didn't want to get trapped belowground.

Hernandez said, "There was no one on this side."

Tynan moved toward the window and looked out. It opened onto a street that led back toward the high mountain and the overhang, but once they were in the street, it might lead to a way out.

There wasn't much time. The sun would be coming up and they needed the cover of darkness to get out. They needed the darkness so that they could get a head start; every minute they delayed meant that the enemy could be flooding the whole area with warriors.

"Okay," said Tynan. "Hernandez, I hate to do this to you, but you've got point."

"I'm truly shocked."

"Jefferson, you'll have to be responsible for the civilians. Keep them together and keep them moving. Lancer, you're with Hernandez and I'll bring up the rear with Jacobs.''

"When?" asked Jacobs.

"Now. Go.''

Hernandez didn't hesitate. He put a foot up on the windowsill and a hand on the side. He pulled himself up and leaped through. He crouched for a moment, his eyes roaming over the shadows and shapes around him. He took off then, trotting down the street. At the corner, he halted and crouched, waiting.

Lancer was right behind him. Jefferson helped Sara Robinson and King through and then followed. As they worked their way toward the corner, Moore and Hughes came through the window.

Tynan moved across the floor, toward the steps that led down into the dungeon. There was no movement there. Jacobs left his post at the doorway and leaped through the window. Tynan followed him and the two men ran after the rest of their group.

As he neared, Hernandez took off again. He trotted down the street, dodged once, and then stopped. The rest of the party followed, stringing out a little bit. Lancer hung back, helping Jefferson get the scientists moving.

In ten minutes they had reached the edge of the city. Hernandez halted there, waiting for Tynan. He pointed at the mountains that surrounded the city and said, "We can go up here, or we could skirt the edge and find an easier climb.''

"Let's find a good place to go up.''

Hernandez nodded and started off again, moving more slowly, listening for the sound of the Mayans in pursuit. But all he could hear were the drums from the pyramid and the cries of the wounded who had fallen in the assault on the house.

He kept going until he came to a large open area. He stopped and moved toward it, sensing something in it. There were walls about four feet high around it and as he peeked over the top, he saw over two hundred men lined up on the open field.

These were more warriors. They wore the padded leather gear and held spears and swords. They stood quietly, waiting for someone to tell them what to do.

Hernandez withdrew quietly. He worked his way to the rear and waved to Lancer, sending him back. When he caught up, he pointed to the north and into the jungle.

Tynan arrived and asked quietly, "What's the problem?"

"They've got about two hundred guys waiting for us up ahead."

Tynan glanced in that direction but could see nothing in front of him. He also realized that it meant they wouldn't be able to get back to the base. He would have to abandon the equipment, just as he had feared. It happened every time.

For a moment he thought about trying to get up the hill to the equipment, but then decided against it. At the very worst, it would be two days before they got back to civilization. Nothing in the equipment stash would shorten that time.

Only getting out of the valley would shorten it.

Without a hesitation, he said, "Then, let's get out of here. Into the jungle. Move off about half a click and then see if we can skirt the city to an easier climb."

"You think that's a good idea, Skipper?"

"Fuck no, but I want to get out of here." He knew that the sun would be coming up in less than an hour and if they were caught in the open it would be a short fight.

"Yes, sir," said Hernandez. He turned and stepped into the jungle.

12

The climb to the top of the ridge had been grueling. It had been a noisy, tiring process. The point had worked to find the best route, but it was still steep, and the need for speed had increased the pressure on them. The three scientists who had been held prisoner were not in the best of shape. Jefferson and Lancer had to help them make it.

And the sounds from the city indicated that a pursuit was being organized. There had been trumpets and shouts and the never-ending beat of the drums. Lights had flickered as torches were lit and it seemed that men were massing on the side of the city where Tynan and his band had been.

Tynan tried to get the people to move faster. He shouted encouragement to them, urging them on, no longer worried about noise discipline because the Mayans seemed to know exactly where they were.

Tynan reached the top of the ridge, breathing hard, the sweat pouring from him. He saw two people spawled on the ground, the breath rasping in their throats. One man stood guard over them and Hernandez was nowhere to be seen. Tynan rushed forward, dropped to one knee, and gasped, ''Where's . . . Hernandez?''

''Checking the route,'' said Lancer.

Tynan nodded and put one hand on his own knee,

forcing himself to stand. He turned and pointed to the rear. "Jacobs, make sure there's no one coming up behind us!"

Jacobs nodded and spun. He hurried to the rear and dropped down, watching the slope. Although he was breathing hard, he tried to remain quiet so that he wouldn't give the enemy a clue as to his location.

Tynan hurried forward and found Hernandez watching the trail. The SEAL turned and said, "Skipper, I'm not sure which way to go."

Tynan knew that the trail would give them the easiest route to follow, but also knew that they had to avoid it. It was a standard combat rule that you never followed the same path twice because if you did, you were asking for an ambush. But that was a combat rule and they weren't in a real combat environment.

Tynan rocked back and pulled out his map. The jungle was just beginning to brighten, but there wasn't enough light to see. He used his flashlight and showed the map to Hernandez. Sweat dripped from his face, snapping against the paper of the map, creating wet spots.

"I think we should avoid the first camp," said Tynan. He pointed to the clearing where they had found the remains of the expedition. "Those guys who passed us on the trail could only be going one place."

"You mean they've set up an ambush there?"

"Yeah. They sent out one group and wiped out the first expedition there. They sent out a second group and ran into us. There has to be a third in the clearing."

Hernandez nodded. "Makes sense."

"So I want to bypass it. Let's make a beeline for the jeeps. That gets us out of here the fastest."

Hernandez examined the map in the dim light of the flashlight. "Going to be rough going for part of the way. Look at the slope of the land."

"Sure," agreed Tynan, "but we can slow down because they won't expect us to do that."

"Unless they just throw out search parties in the hopes of stumbling across us."

"But they're working against the clock. They've only got a few hours to find us and then we're out of here. They can't pursue us too far."

Jacobs came to them. "We better get going. They're coming up the hill."

"You know what to do," Tynan told Hernandez. "Give us three minutes and then get going."

Tynan joined Jacobs and they rushed back to the main body. Tynan stopped long enough to order Jefferson and Lancer to get the people moving. He told them to catch up with Hernandez.

With that done, Jacobs and Tynan ran to the edge of the hill. Below them they could hear the Mayans fighting their way up the slope. Tynan crouched near the trunk of a large tree, staring into the dimness of the jungle. He flipped his weapon off safety, and wished that he had a couple hand grenades. If he could toss them down the hill, it would slow the pursuit.

Around him the jungle was coming alive. Birds were screaming and monkeys were yelling. There were roars and chirps and screams. And there were the drums, rumbling in the distance.

Tynan stretched out on his belly, watching for movement. He could hear the Mayans crashing through the jungle. There were grunts and orders. He aimed at the sound and fired a short burst. The rounds snapped through air, stripping leaves and bark from the trees.

From below there were shouts and screams. It sounded as if the Mayans were scrambling for cover. Tynan fired again. Birds took off and monkeys shrieked. And then there was silence. Except for the drums.

Tynan glanced to the right. "Let's go. That should slow them down."

They got to their feet and took off after the others. They ran through the jungle, dodging the bushes and trees and depressions. They listened to the animals around them, listened for clues that the enemy was coming, but heard nothing.

They reached a narrow stream and stopped. Tynan dropped to his knees and threw the cool water on his face. He dunked his head and then leaped to the other side. Jacobs joined him there.

"Now what?"

"We keep going."

"Maybe we should hang back and ambush them again. That might discourage pursuit."

Tynan thought about it. There was some merit to the idea, though he was worried about pursuers using other paths—Mayans who were already in the jungle and who could be lying in wait. He didn't want to delay too long.

"No," he said. "We need to catch the others."

Then, almost as if to underscore his words, there was a burst of firing in the distance. Two or three M16's on full auto. Quick bursts and then nothing.

Jacobs glanced at Tynan.

"Got to believe they just shot their way clear. Let's get going."

Tynan took point, running through the jungle. He leaped over obstacles, ignoring the noise he was making. He angled to the right and then stopped, listening, but heard nothing new. He rushed on again, until he came to a huge outcropping of rock, where he halted.

As Jacobs joined him, he moved off again, working his way around the rocks. On the far side, he waited. He took a drink from his canteen, spitting the warm water on the ground, trying to wash the cotton from his mouth.

When Jacobs caught up, Tynan started running again, holding his weapon in both hands, the safety on. He listened to the sounds of the jungle, but heard nothing unusual.

Then, from a clump of bushes to the right, he heard a quiet groaning. He slid to a halt, crouched, and turned, snapping off the safety. When Jacobs joined him, he pointed to the left and then back to the right where the groaning had come from.

Slowly, with Jacobs covering him, he worked his way to the clump of bushes. When he reached it, he hesitated and then entered it. Inside he found one dead man, a bullet wound in the center of his chest. Next to him was the wounded, groaning man. A bullet had smashed his leg. He lay with his bloodstained hands wrapped around his wounded appendage, moaning. There wasn't much blood and Tynan was sure the man would survive. He just wouldn't walk again.

He returned to Jacobs and the two of them started off again. Now the jungle was quiet except for the animals and the sound of their ragged breathing as the two men ran. The Mayans were not closing in on them, at least from the rear.

Five minutes later they caught up to Hernandez and his party. The SEALS had taken up defensive positions, surrounding the scientists, who were lying around, breathing hard.

Tynan found Hernandez and asked, "What happened back there?"

"Ran into about five of the enemy. Came at us with swords and we had to shoot. A couple of them went down and the others ran."

"Any of our people hurt?"

"No, sir. They're just worn out. Had to let them rest. They're not used to this."

Tynan dropped to the ground and pulled out his map. He examined it carefully, searching for landmarks around him—the stream that they had crossed; the rock outcropping and the slope of the land. He figured they had made two, maybe three clicks from the city, but they still had a long way to go.

"Let's get this show on the road," said Tynan. "Slowly this time. We don't want to run into anything."

Hernandez got to his feet and studied the map for a moment. He looked into the distance and checked his compass. "I'm ready whenever you are."

Tynan returned to the main body and got the people on their feet. He noticed that Sara Robinson didn't look good. Her face was pale and she seemed to be on the edge of hysteria, but there was nothing he could do about it, except watch her. King, on the other hand, seemed ready for a fight. It made an interesting contrast.

They moved out slowly, working their way through the undergrowth, which was thick for a short distance and then seemed to disappear as the trees got taller and the canopy overhead cut down the amount of sunlight getting through. That meant that the undergrowth was thinning out, in some places looking like a well-kept park.

They kept moving as the heat of the day built. By midmorning they were covered with sweat and the pace had slowed. The civilians were having a tough time keeping up with the SEALS. None of them had the stamina of the Navy men, and they had been treated roughly during their stay in the Mayan prison.

But Tynan wouldn't let them rest. He kept them moving, telling them that by the end of the day, if they kept at it, they could be eating dinner in an air conditioned restaurant and, for a time, that was enough incentive.

Around them the jungle remained quiet. The semi-dense vegetation was their friend. It didn't make travel impossible, but it did offer a certain amount of concealment. Tynan was happy to be where he was.

At noon he ordered a halt, realizing that if he kept pressing, the civilians would collapse and have to be carried. The SEALS spread out, forming a tiny perimeter so that they could watch the jungle for the pursuit that didn't seem to be forming. They drank their water in small sips and ate food that was heavily salted.

They rested a short time and then Tynan moved Lancer to point and told Hernandez to help Jefferson with the scientists. He gave Lancer a compass course and cautioned him not to range too far to the front.

Again they moved out, staying away from the trails because they figured the Mayans would scatter people all over them. By moving cross-country, they reduced the chance that they would run into some of the enemy.

They made good time, stopping to drench themselves whenever they encountered a stream, and resting every hour or so. They shed most of the equipment they still carried. Tynan wished that they had been able to get back to where they had dropped their packs, but that couldn't be helped.

It was about three in the afternoon when Lancer turned and came back to the main party. Tynan worked his way to the man and crouched near him.

"I think we've got a problem, Skipper. There are a couple of dozen warriors in front of us."

"Can we get around them?"

"Not easily. They picked the best place to wait for us." Lancer took out his map and pointed. "See the way the valley deepens here. It's no more than a couple hundred meters across. They're strung out from one side to the other. We try to pull an end run and we add seven, eight clicks at a minimum."

Tynan took the map and studied it. He hadn't noticed the way the valley narrowed. It then blossomed outward until it was miles across. Once they had reached that area, they would turn to the north and in four or five clicks, at the most, they would be at the jeeps.

Tynan studied the map, looking for a way out. He knew that he couldn't retreat. Even though they had heard no one behind them for hours, he had to assume they were there. Even the poorest trackers had to be able to follow their trail. Tynan's only real advantage was that the Mayans didn't have radio. To find them across their path could only mean that the Mayans had put a thousand people into the jungle.

The ridges on either side of the valley were a thousand feet high. They were fairly gentle slopes in most places, but the lay of the land meant that there was no easy way around the roadblock.

"How much ammo you got?" asked Tynan.

Lancer didn't have to check. He knew. "Four magazines for the rifle and three for the pistol."

"Little more than I have."

Jefferson chimed in. "I've got six magazines for the M16 and three for the pistol." He shrugged. "I didn't have much of a chance to shoot."

Tynan was quiet for a moment. "All right, we'll try to sneak by them. If not, we'll shoot our way past."

"Sir," said Moore. "I appreciate all you're doing for us, but don't you think that it would be better to negotiate?"

"Dr. Moore," said Tynan, shaking his head, "these people are not interested in negotiations. You watched them cut the throats of two of your people and you saw what they did to your expedition in the field."

Moore kept his eyes on the ground. "Yes, I know that. I just think that we should try to negotiate."

"Your suggestion is duly noted."

"And ignored."

Tynan turned so that he could stare at the scientist. "Are you seriously suggesting that we try to talk to these people?"

There was a hesitation and then Moore said, "No. Not really. I just thought someone should bring it up."

"Any other suggestions?"

"Wait until dark?" said Jacobs, who had moved closer.

"Not with the civilians. We've got to get through there. Otherwise I'd wait."

"How soon?"

Tynan turned and studied the scientists. They looked beat. Tired, sweaty, and dirty. Moore and Hughes looked strong enough. Tynan had seen enough of King to know that she could keep up and she could be fairly quiet. It was Robinson who was the unknown quantity. She could make the mistake that would get them all killed. It could be a little thing.

Tynan leaned close to Jefferson. "I want you to stay with Robinson. Help her."

"Aye, aye, sir."

"Okay, let's check our weapons and get rid of anything that will rattle or make noise. Move out in five minutes, and once we do, no one talks."

Tynan then moved around the tiny perimeter, checking on everyone, making sure that the instructions were understood. Once he had finished that, he told Lancer he would take point. He checked the map one last time and then began to move toward the Mayans.

For the first hundred meters, he wasn't worried. Then, as he neared the place where the Mayans waited, he slowed, making sure of each step, avoiding the dry twigs and leaves. He stepped around problems and let his eyes search for the enemy.

He came to an area where the sunlight streamed through the canopy. He stopped short of it and used his binoculars to search the forest. In the distance he spotted a single man standing next to a tree, looking like a guard at a palace gate. He held a spear in his left hand and wore the leather padding that meant he was a soldier.

Slowly, he checked the rest of the valley floor. There was a man five feet to the left of the warrior by the tree, and a third near a bush. They had strung out across the floor at about a double-arm interval. There didn't seem to be a way to sneak by them.

If there were a way to take out one man, leaving a wider gap, then they might make it without a fight. But as it was, they would have to shoot their way through.

And then, almost as if one of the Mayans had heard his thoughts, the man leaned his spear against the tree to answer the call of nature. There was no time to hesitate. No time to brief the others.

Tynan slung his rifle, pulled his knife, and started forward, watching the other guards. He dropped to the ground, crawling forward, hoping that the Mayan would take his time. He reached the tree and glanced right and left, but both those men were staring into the trees.

He inched forward and just as he was ready to attack, the man appeared. Tynan stood to meet him. He grabbed the man's head putting a hand over his nose and mouth. As he did, he struck with his knife, slashing at the throat. There was a splash of hot wet blood and a whiff of bowel. The Mayan sagged and Tynan went with him, trying to keep him from falling noisily to the ground and warning the others.

Tynan spun away from the body. As he moved, there was a cry of surprise. Another of the guards shouted something and Tynan knew he had failed. He threw his knife and watched as it buried itself in the chest of the warrior, who staggered to the rear. One hand grasped the knife ineffectually as he fell to his butt. He sat there, blood pumping from his wound, his face turning waxy. A moment later he rolled to the side, dying with one hand on the knife.

As the man died, the third guard spun. He saw the bodies sprawled on the ground, covered with blood, and then spotted Tynan. A roar bubbled in his throat and he lowered his head to charge, the point of his spear held low.

Tynan rolled to his left and clawed at the holster. He whipped his pistol out, aiming at the charging man. The warrior kept coming, never looking up at him. Tynan fired as the pistol cleared the holster. The round took the Mayan in the chin, shattering it. Blood spurted and the man collapsed, both hands on his face. He lost his spear as he rolled from side to side, screaming in pain.

Firing rippled from the right. Tynan dived to the side,

and rolled toward the tree. He came up on one knee and aimed, but there was no one to see. He heard bullets snapping through the jungle. He put his pistol into his holster and pulled his rifle from his shoulder. He checked it for dirt and debris, and then slipped off the safety.

There was movement to the right and Tynan turned to face it. He saw a flash of color, but didn't fire because he didn't know if it was the enemy or not. He waited and watched, and when the man appeared again, Tynan was ready. He aimed at a point behind the ear and fired. The Mayan warrior flipped over, his feet drumming on the ground. His legs worked, pushing him into the jungle as he screamed in pain. There was a gurgling groan and then nothing.

Tynan crouched again, waiting. The firing increased and one man was shooting on full auto. There were shouts and cries and a few words in English. The firing stopped suddenly and there were only the echoes of it mixed with the calls of animals and the distant drums of the city. And then it came again. A sudden burst of a single weapon.

Tynan heard a crashing in the jungle near him and whirled. Three of the Mayans ran from the cover there, each holding a spear. Tynan opened fire, pulling the trigger quickly. One man went down immediately. He rolled over and tripped one of those with him. Tynan shot the last of the trio and then turned his attention on the man who had tripped.

That man stood staring down the barrel of Tynan's weapon and made no move. He had forgotten about his spear. He had forgotten about killing the invaders. He was frozen, his eyes wide in terror.

Tynan knew what he should do. The enemy deserved no mercy. You killed enemy soldiers because if you didn't, they would come back and kill you later. History was full of that lesson. Mercy granted that was turned against the man who had been merciful. But Tynan couldn't pull the trigger. The man had no idea what he was up against. The man was only doing what he had been told to do and it was bad luck that had put him in danger.

It hung like that for a moment. Neither man moving, the battle raging around them. Firing to the right and left. Bullets slamming through the jungle. The cries of frightened animals and birds and the shouts of the wounded.

The warrior got to his feet slowly, his eyes never moving from Tynan's. He held his hands out, palms down, away from his body. He ignored the bodies of the men near him. Ignored the spears. Instead, he took a step to the rear and when Tynan didn't react, the man spun. He fled into the jungle, dodging right and left as if to make himself a hard to hit target.

With that, Tynan began to move to the rear. He kept his eyes moving, listening to the sounds of the shooting. Through a gap in the trees, he spotted Jefferson kneeling, firing his weapon into the jungle.

Tynan turned and saw three of the enemy soldiers. He dropped to one knee and aimed, but the men were not attacking. They were trying to drag a wounded Mayan out of the field of fire. Again Tynan had a man in his sights and again he refused to pull the trigger. He couldn't see any of these men being a threat to him now, he was too close to getting out. And then he wondered if he was getting soft.

But then another of the Mayans appeared, his spear held high. Tynan watched him run at Jefferson like a linebacker coming up on the blind side of the quarterback. Tynan didn't hesitate. He fired once. As his bullet snapped by Jefferson's head, the SEAL dived to his right.

Tynan fired again but the target had dropped into the jungle. Tynan was up then, moving toward Jefferson, his eyes searching for the enemy warrior. As he approached, he saw the body lying in the verdant vegetation, the blood staining it crimson.

Jefferson glanced at Tynan and said, "Thanks, Skipper."

"No problem."

As he crouched next to Jefferson, the firing began to taper off until it was sporadic, single shots. Tynan searched the jungle, but could see no sign of the enemy now.

"Cease fire!" he ordered and then stood.

Jacobs appeared to the right and moved toward them. His uniform was torn and splashed with blood.

"You hit?" asked Tynan.

"Huh?" said Jacobs. He glanced at himself and then grunted. "No. It's not mine."

Lancer and Hernandez appeared, along with the civilians. Tynan pointed to the rear and Lancer broke off, taking a position to cover them, if they needed it.

"Anyone hurt in the fight?" He waited and then asked the question again. This time Jefferson shook his head. "We're all fine, Skipper."

As the men gathered again, Tynan glanced at his watch, surprised that an hour had been used in the fight. He would have guessed it at ten minutes at the most. He checked the position of the sun, sure that they could get clear before nightfall.

Tynan pointed to the front and said, "Jacobs take point. Let's get moving."

"Aye, aye, sir," said Jacobs. He moved into the forest, glanced at the body of a dead warrior and kept going.

"How far?" asked Moore.

Tynan shook his head and said, "No more than three, four hours, if we don't run into anything else."

"That's good," said Moore. "I'm not sure how much farther we can go without some rest."

"I know what you mean," said Tynan. "I'm getting worn out, too, but we've got to get clear before nightfall."

"I understand. I was just letting you know the situation."

Tynan didn't respond to that. He knew exactly what the situation was. They had burned most of their ammo in the fight and if they ran into another large party of Mayans, that would be it. The only thing they could do now was work their way through the jungle as quickly as possible before the Mayans could mount a pursuit.

"Keep me informed," said Tynan. But he hoped that they would be out of the jungle before Moore said anything to him.

13

Tynan had wanted to get out of the valley as quickly as possible. If nothing else, the sound of the gunfire would have to act like a magnet, drawing everyone who could hear in that direction. Then, as he was trying to get everyone organized again, Lancer approached.

"Skipper, there is someone coming up behind us."

"Well, shit. That tears it. Let's get out of here now."

Jacobs moved rapidly, fading into the jungle. As he disappeared, Tynan ordered, "Jefferson. Get these people moving. Lancer, Hernandez, you're with me."

Jefferson hesitated. Moore was on his feet and moving, dragging Robinson with him. Hughes and King followed with Jefferson right behind them, covering them.

When they were out of sight, Tynan tapped Hernandez and pointed to the right. "Five meters. Lancer, on the other side about the same place. And then we retreat."

Just as Lancer reached his position, Tynan heard a crash in the jungle about twenty or thirty meters away. He could see nothing but didn't like the sound of it. He waved at the men and they began their coordinated withdrawal.

There was a second crash and Tynan was suddenly reminded of the beaters on an African lion hunt. Men with long poles beating them on the ground to drive the animals in a certain direction. What he didn't know was whether the beaters wanted them to attack or retreat, if they were beaters.

He glanced to the right and saw that Hernandez was moving steadily. Lancer was doing fine on the left. Tynan kept backing up, waiting for someone to appear, but that didn't happen. There was just the noise, as if something large were attacking them.

For a moment he thought about stopping and letting the Mayans catch up, but then decided to avoid another contact. Instead he yelled, "Let's get the fuck out of here."

With that he spun and began to trot. He jumped over a rotting log and kept going. He saw that both the other SEALS were keeping pace with him. And then he realized that the beaters were falling behind. The crashes weren't as loud as they had been. They were being cautious and that gave Tynan the advantage he needed. He increased his pace.

And then suddenly, they were out of the valley. The steep cliffs that had boxed them in were gone, replaced by the jungle. The vegetation thinned, too, making travel easier. Far in front, he could see the rear of their tiny formation. Jefferson was keeping the scientists moving, but Tynan and the two SEALS were moving faster.

"Okay, let's take five." He slipped to one knee near the gigantic trunk of a fallen tree. He leaned back against it, listening. In the far distance he could hear the beaters and beyond them, coming from the city, was the sound of drumming. A very faint sound now. A subliminal sound that added a sense of danger to the jungle.

After seven minutes, Tynan was up again. The others followed him. They jogged along, leaped a narrow, shallow stream, and found where the others had turned toward the north. Now they were heading straight for the jeeps. Two, three clicks and they would be there.

Tynan stopped long enough to listen for the enemy. If they were trying to drive Tynan and his people in one direction, they were failing. The sound was barely audible and seemed to be following the original path. They hadn't realized that Tynan's group had changed direction.

Lancer, the breath rasping in his throat asked, "What happened?"

"I think," said Tynan, "they expected us to continue down the valley. We fooled them with the change of direction."

"Then, we can slow down."

"Not until we catch the first group."

Lancer shrugged and wiped the sweat from his face. "You're the boss."

Again they took off, jogging along. Twenty minutes later they found the rear of the formation and hurried to catch up. Jefferson saw them coming and halted the rest.

"How are we doing?" he asked.

"We gave them the slip. All we have to do is reach the jeeps and we're home free."

"Unless they found them first and are waiting for us there," said Lancer.

"Christ," said Tynan, "I wish you hadn't said that."

"Well, I like to try and look at the bright side," responded Lancer. He grinned and added, "Spread a little rain into everyone's life."

Tynan moved past everyone and found Jacobs. He looked at the map then and said, "What? A click, maybe less."

"Or a little more. We're real close."

"Okay. Let's stay here for fifteen minutes and then make the last leg in one jump."

"Aye, aye, sir."

Tynan moved to the rear and told the scientists, "I make it about a click to the jeeps. An hour at best over fairly flat terrain. You people going to be able to make it?"

Moore laughed. "You have jeeps?"

"With room enough for everyone to ride. Might be a little crowded, but we do have jeeps."

"Then, yes, we can make it."

"We'll go in about ten minutes."

Tynan returned to the rear. He crouched there and used his binoculars. He scanned the jungle but there was nothing to see. He listened intently, but there was nothing to hear. When ten minutes was up, he put the binoculars away and turned. He took a rearguard position, thinking that it was going too easily again. There had to be something wrong.

But there wasn't. The jungle had thinned and they made better time than he had expected. They burst from it and Tynan saw Jefferson and the scientists standing on the muddy road. Jacobs was about thirty meters away, crouched by the side of the road, watching for the Mayans. As soon as Tynan had joined the main body, Jacobs started out again.

Now Tynan expected the jeeps to be missing, or that the Mayans had found them and destroyed them. He expected to find all the tires flat or the gas leaking onto the ground. His mind was filled with a hundred things that could be wrong, but when they located the jeeps, he learned that he had worried for nothing.

As Tynan walked up to them, Jacobs was sitting in the passenger seat. King was behind the wheel, fumbling for her keys. Before Tynan got too close, she had started the engine. It took a moment to catch and then coughed once, but then it smoothed out, running quietly.

Tynan stopped dead in his tracks. For an instant the scientists were quiet and then Hughes let out a whoop. The others began cheering, slapping each other on the back as Tynan realized that the mission was basically over. He rushed to the running jeep, leaned in, and kissed King on the lips.

She grinned and said, "Why, Lieutenant, I didn't think you cared."

Three days later Tynan sat in a large conference room and listened to the story told by Moore. He listened to

King confirm nearly everything and then was asked for his opinion. He told them that he didn't feel qualified to comment on the subject.

"That's all right, Lieutenant," said Moffit, running the whole show as he had the last time Tynan had been in Washington at one of these meetings. "I just want to know the accuracy of the statements made by the scientists."

"In that case, I think it's fair to say that the city is still inhabited by descendants of the Mayans. I don't pretend to understand how they managed to escape detection, and I'll grant that my contact with them was limited to a night recon, but I think Drs. Moore and King are representing it fairly."

"Then it becomes a question of what we should do about it," said Moffit.

"What we do," said Moore, "is return better prepared. We study these people fully because of what they can tell us of the Mayans. Granted, their society will have been polluted by contact with the outside world, but we have an unique opportunity here. It's not unlike the situation that Cortés found when he landed in the New World."

"We'll have to protect those people," agreed Moffit.

"Aren't we making a slight error here?" said King. "Those people, as you call them, do not live in the United States. It's a foreign nation."

"But the important thing," added Moore, "is that we protect them. If word of this gets out too quickly, then the opportunity will be lost."

Tynan could see the direction that the debate was taking. A scientific discussion on how to best protect and exploit the discovery. Who would get what credit when the scientific papers were written. They didn't want to hear about his role in the rescue, and, in fact, ignored the role the military had played in getting the people out.

Finally he stood and said, "If you have no further questions for me . . ."

Moffit smiled. "No, Lieutenant, I think we've finished

with you. Please remember that everything discussed in here, and everything you've seen in the last few days, is considered classified material.''

Tynan felt like telling the man that you couldn't classify scientific knowledge, and that the various levels of classification had been designed for information that helped protect the national security, but he didn't. Instead, he told them that he would keep it in mind. He didn't mention that he had told everything he knew during the normal debriefing the Navy had held on his return.

He left the room as Moore and Moffit argued about who would publish what, and when and how they could mount more expeditions into the region. He knew that within five years, the society that he had glimpsed would be destroyed. Hell, it was already too late to save them. They had seen flashlights and rifles and a hundred other devices from the modern world. They could see the airplanes flying overhead. The contact had contaminated them and that couldn't be reversed. Having glimpsed the candy store, the Mayans would want to enter it as quickly as possible.

But then, none of that was his worry. He had done his job quickly and efficiently, and he didn't understand the sadness he felt. Maybe it was because he knew that he had ruined a way of life. Maybe it was because he felt sorry that the Mayans were going to enter the modern world. Or maybe it was just a sadness at the way the supposedly civilized people were fighting to cut up a pie that belonged to someone else.

There was nothing he could do about it. Any protest he lodged would be referred to the people in the conference room and they would do nothing about it.

He hit the button for the elevator again, wondering who was holding it up. He wanted out of the building. Out into the sunshine of Washington, D.C., where he could forget about high-level decisions made in self-interest rather than out of compassion for those who would be affected, especially when those affected had no voice in the government.

There was a sound behind him and he turned. Stephanie King was walking down the hallway. She was dressed in a white blouse and a short black skirt. She looked much better than she had running through the jungles of Honduras, but then, everyone he knew looked better, even Sara Robinson, who had improved dramatically when they had left Central America.

"Mark," said King as she neared him, "I was afraid that I would miss you."

"Get tired of sitting there listening to all that?" he asked, pointing back at the conference room.

"Yes. Tired and sick. I had to get out. Thought maybe I could buy you something to eat."

The elevator arrived with a ding of the bell and a rumble of sliding doors. Tynan reached out and put his hand against the rubber to keep them open.

"Something to eat," he repeated. "Yeah, I think that I could be convinced to go to dinner."

She entered the elevator and Tynan followed. He punched the button for the ground floor.

"I've been wanting to tell you that I think you did a terrific job down there in Honduras. We'd never have been able to . . . ah, get out of there if it hadn't been for your expertise. I learned a lot about the role of the military."

Tynan shrugged. "I was just doing what I had been ordered to do."

"Well, anyway, thanks." She stepped back and leaned against the rear wall and grinned. "So we'll have dinner and then figure out something else to do."

"I think we'll think of something to do after dinner." He returned her smile, reaching for her.

SEALS

by Steve Mackenzie

**THE WORLD'S MOST RUTHLESS
FIGHTING UNIT,
TAKING THE ART OF WARFARE
TO THE LIMIT — AND BEYOND!**

SEALS #1: AMBUSH!	75189-5/$2.95US/$3.95Can
SEALS #2: BLACKBIRD	75190-9/$2.50US/$3.50Can
SEALS #3: RESCUE!	75191-7/$2.50US/$3.50Can
SEALS #4: TARGET!	75193-3/$2.95US/$3.95Can
SEALS #5: BREAKOUT!	75194-1/$2.95US/$3.95Can
SEALS #6: DESERT RAID	75195-X/$2.95US/$3.95Can
SEALS #7: RECON	75529-7/$2.95US/$3.95Can

*and more exciting action adventure
coming soon from Avon Books*

SEALS #8: INFILTRATE!	75530-0/$2.95US/$3.95Can
SEALS #9:	75532-7/$2.95US/$3.95Can